FALLEN INK - SPECIAL EDITION
MONTGOMERY INK: COLORADO SPRINGS

CARRIE ANN RYAN

Fallen Ink
A Montgomery Ink: Colorado Springs Novel
By: Carrie Ann Ryan
© 2018 Carrie Ann Ryan

This book is a work of fiction. Names, characters, places, and incidents either are products of the author's imagination or are used fictitiously. Any resemblance to actual events, locales or persons, living or dead, is entirely coincidental.

No part of this book can be reproduced in any form or by electronic or mechanical means including information storage and retrieval systems, without the express written permission of the author. The only exception is by a reviewer who may quote short excerpts in a review.

All content warnings are listed on the book page for this book on my website.

NO AI TRAINING: Without in any way limiting the author's [and publisher's] exclusive rights under copyright, any use of this publication to "train" generative artificial intelligence (AI) technologies to generate text is expressly prohibited. The author reserves all rights to license uses of this work for generative AI training and development of machine learning language models.

PRAISE FOR CARRIE ANN RYAN....

"One of the best family romance series around! Carrie Ann Ryan brings the heat, emotions, and love in each story!" ~ NYT Bestselling Author Corinne Michaels

"Count on Carrie Ann Ryan for emotional, sexy, character driven stories that capture your heart!" – Carly Phillips, NY Times bestselling author

"Carrie Ann Ryan's romances are my newest addiction! The emotion in her books captures me from the very beginning. The hope and healing hold me close until the end. These love stories will simply sweep you away." ~ NYT Bestselling Author Deveny Perry

"Carrie Ann Ryan writes the perfect balance of sweet and heat ensuring every story feeds the soul." - Audrey Carlan, #1 New York Times Bestselling Author

"Carrie Ann Ryan never fails to draw readers in with

passion, raw sensuality, and characters that pop off the page. Any book by Carrie Ann is an absolute treat." – New York Times Bestselling Author J. Kenner

"Carrie Ann Ryan knows how to pull your heartstrings and make your pulse pound! Her wonderful Redwood Pack series will draw you in and keep you reading long into the night. I can't wait to see what comes next with the new generation, the Talons. Keep them coming, Carrie Ann!" –Lara Adrian, New York Times bestselling author of CRAVE THE NIGHT

"With snarky humor, sizzling love scenes, and brilliant, imaginative worldbuilding, The Dante's Circle series reads as if Carrie Ann Ryan peeked at my personal wish list!" – NYT Bestselling Author, Larissa Ione

"Carrie Ann Ryan writes sexy shifters in a world full of passionate happily-ever-afters." – *New York Times* Bestselling Author Vivian Arend

"Carrie Ann's books are sexy with characters you can't help but love from page one. They are heat and heart blended to perfection." *New York Times* Bestselling Author Jayne Rylon

Carrie Ann Ryan's books are wickedly funny and deliciously hot, with plenty of twists to keep you guessing. They'll keep you up all night!" USA Today Bestselling Author Cari Quinn

"Once again, Carrie Ann Ryan knocks the Dante's Circle series out of the park. The queen of hot, sexy, enthralling paranormal romance, Carrie Ann is an author not to miss!" *New York Times* bestselling Author Marie Harte

ACKNOWLEDGMENTS

I was so excited to dive into more of the Montgomery Ink world. I knew the story wasn't over in Denver, so now we've headed south to Colorado Springs!

I want to thank my team for each of their parts in this book. I know I couldn't do this without them.

Thank you, readers, for making Montgomery Ink what it is and I hope you love these new characters as much as I do!

And before I go, I have to thank Dr. Hubby. He was so happy for me when I said I wanted to write these characters and while I'm still broken he can't be here to see it complete, I know he's watching over us and laughing along with Mace and Adrienne.

Happy Reading,

~Carrie Ann

FALLEN INK

The Montgomery Ink series continues with a spin-off in Colorado Springs, where a familiar Montgomery finds her place in a new tattoo shop, and in the arms of her best friend.

Adrienne Montgomery is finally living her dreams. She's opened a tattoo shop with her brother, Shep, and two of her cousins from Denver and she's ready to take the city by storm with her art—as long as she can handle the pressure. When her new neighbors decide her shop isn't a great fit for the community, however, she'll have to lean on the one person she didn't expect to fall for along the way…her best friend.

Mace Knight takes pride in two things: his art and his daughter. He knows he's taking a risk by starting over in a new shop with the Montgomerys, but the stakes are even higher when he finds himself wanting Adrienne more than he thought possible.

The two fall fast and hard but they know the rules; they can't risk their friendship, no matter how hot it is between the sheets and how many people try to stand in their way.

CHAPTER ONE

Adrienne Montgomery wasn't going to throw up, but it would probably be a close call. It wasn't that she was a nervous person, but today of all days was bound to test her patience and nerves, and she wasn't sure if all those years of growing a spine of steel would be enough.

Maybe she should have worked on forming a steel-lined gut while she was at it—perhaps even a platinum one.

"You're looking pretty pale over there," Mace said, leaning down low to whisper in her ear.

She shivered involuntarily as his breath slid across her neck, and she looked up into her best friend's hazel gaze. The damn man was far too handsome for his own good, and he *knew* she was ticklish, so he constantly spoke in her ear so she shivered like that.

She figured he'd gotten a haircut the day before because the sides were close-cut so you could see the white in his salt-and-pepper hair. He'd let the top grow out, and he had it brushed to the side so it actually looked a little fashionable rather than messy and just hanging in his eyes like most days. Knowing Mace, he'd done it by accident that morning, rather than making it a point to do so. Her best friend was around her age, in his thirties, but had gone salt-and-pepper in his late twenties. While some men might have started dyeing their hair, Mace had made it work with his ink and piercings—and the ladies liked it.

Well, at least that's what Adrienne figured. It wasn't as if she were one of his following. Not in that way, at least.

"Yo, Adrienne, you okay?"

She glowered, hearing the familiar refrain that had been the bane of her existence since she was in kindergarten and one of the fathers there had shouted it like the boxer from that movie she now hated.

"What did I say about using that phrase?" She crossed her arms over her chest and tapped her foot. She was at least six inches shorter than her best friend, but since she was wearing her heeled boots, she could at least try to look intimidating.

Mace being Mace just shrugged and winked, giving her that smolder that he'd practiced in the mirror after seeing *Tangled* with her years ago. Yeah, he was *that* guy, the one who liked to make her smile and knew she had a crush on the animated Flynn Rider.

"You know you like it." He wrapped an arm around her shoulder and gave her a tight squeeze. "Now, are you okay? Really? Because you honestly look like you're about to throw up, and with the place all new and shiny, I don't know if vomit really sets the tone."

Thinking about the reason the place—*her* place— was all new and shiny sent her stomach into another roll, and she let out a long breath.

"I'm fine."

Mace just stared at her, and she kicked his shoe. Mature, that was her name. "Try it with a little more enthusiasm, because while I'd *like* to believe you, the panic in your eyes doesn't really portray the right confidence."

"I'll *be* fine. How's that?" she asked and gave him a wide smile. It must have looked a little manic, though, since he winced. But he gave her a thumbs up.

"Okay, then. Let's get out of this office and go out into your brand new tattoo shop to meet the horde."

There went her stomach again.

Her tattoo shop.

She couldn't quite believe it. After years of working for others in Colorado Springs instead of going up north to Denver to work at her cousins' shop, or even south to New Orleans and her brother's former shop, she was now part-owner of Montgomery Ink Too, the first offshoot of the main shop in downtown Denver.

Yep, she was going to be sick.

"It's mostly family. Not quite a horde." Sort of, at least. Even three people felt like a lot at this point since they'd all be there…waiting for her to say something, do something, *be* someone. And that was enough of that, or she really wouldn't make it out of the office that day.

"True, since most of your family didn't come. The entire Montgomery clan would probably fill four buildings at this point."

"You're not wrong. Only Austin and Maya came down from Denver since Shep and I asked the others to stay home. It would be a little too much for our small building if everyone showed up."

"But your sisters and parents are here, plus Shep and his wife, of course, and I'm pretty sure I saw their baby Livvy out there, too. And then Ryan, since you hired him." Mace stuffed his hands into his pockets. "It's one big, happy family, who happen to be waiting for you to go out there and possibly start a tattoo a bit later for your first client."

After what had seemed like months of paperwork and construction, today was opening day for Montgomery Ink Too—MIT for short. Ryan and Mace had called it that one day, and the nickname had stuck. There was nothing she could do now but go with it, weirdness and all. There had been delays and weather issues, but *finally*, the shop was open. Now, she needed to be an adult and go out into the main room to socialize.

And there went her stomach again.

Mace's strong arms came around her, and she rested her head on his chest, tucking herself under his chin. He had to lift his head a bit so she could fit since she wasn't *that* short, but it was a familiar position for them. No matter what anyone said about Mace, he gave *great* hugs.

"You're going to be fine." His voice rumbled over her, and she could feel the vibrations through his chest and against her cheek.

"You say that now, but what if everything tumbles down and I end up with no clients and ruin the fact that Austin and Maya trusted me with their first satellite shop."

Austin and Maya were two of her numerous Denver

cousins. There were eight freaking siblings in that family, and all of them had married off—with Maya having *two* husbands even—so it added up to way too many people for her to count. Maya and Austin owned and operated Montgomery Ink in downtown Denver—what was now the flagship shop it seemed.

Her cousins had come to her over a year ago, saying they were interested in expanding the business. Since real estate was sparse off the 16th Street Mall where Montgomery Ink was located, they'd come up with the idea of opening a new tattoo shop in a different city. And wasn't it nice that they had two other artists in the family so close? Well, Shep hadn't actually been close at the time since he was still living in New Orleans where he'd met his wife and started his family, but now her big brother was back in Colorado Springs and was here to stay.

Maya and Austin were still the main owners of the business and CEOs of the corporation they'd formed in order to add on, but Shep and Adrienne had bought into the franchise and were now partial owners *and* managers of Montgomery Ink Too.

That was a lot of responsibility on her shoulders, but she knew she could do it. She just had to buck up and actually walk into the tattoo shop.

"Stop freaking out, Addi. I wouldn't have come with

you on this journey if I didn't believe in you." He pulled away and met her gaze, the intensity so great that she had to blink a few times so she could catch her breath.

He was right. He'd given up a lot for her. Though, in the end, the whole arrangement might work out better for him. Hopefully. He'd left a steady job at their old shop to come and work with her. The trust in that action was staggering, and it gave Adrienne the final bit of strength she needed to do this—whatever *this* was.

"Okay, let's do this."

He held out his hand, and she took it, giving it a squeeze before letting go. It wasn't as if she needed to brace herself against him again or hold his hand as they made their way into the shop. Enough people already wondered just what went on behind closed doors between the two of them. She didn't need to add fuel to the fire.

Mace was just her best friend, nothing more—though certainly nothing less.

He was at her back as she walked through her office door and into the main room, the heat of him keeping her steady. The shop in Colorado Springs matched the one up north in layout, with only a few minor changes. Each station had its own cubicle area, but once people made it past the front section of the shop where onlookers couldn't peep in, it was almost all open. There were two private rooms in the back for those who wanted tattoos that required a little less clothing, as well as folding panels that could be placed in each of the artist's areas so they could be sectioned off easily. Most people didn't mind having other artists and clients watch them while they got a tattoo, and it usually added to the overall experience. As the licensed piercer in residence, Adrienne could do that part of her job in either of the rooms in the back, as well.

While some shops had closed-off rooms for each artist because the building was a converted home or office building, the Montgomerys hadn't wanted that. There was privacy when needed and socialization when desired. It was a great setup, and one Adrienne had been jealous of when she was working at her old place on the other side of the city.

"About time you made your way back here," Maya said dryly, her eyebrow ring glinting under the overhead light.

Adrienne flipped her cousin off then grinned as Maya did the same back. Of all her cousins, she and Maya looked the most alike. They each had long, dark hair, were average height, and had just the right amount of curves to make finding jeans difficult. Of course, Maya had birthed two kids, while Adrienne's butt came from her love of cookies...but that was neither here nor there.

Everyone stood around talking to one another, cups of water or coffee or tea in their hands as they looked around the place. As they weren't opening up for tattoos until later in the day, they were able to easily socialize in the main entry area. Their new hire, Ryan, stood off to the side, and Mace went over to him so they would be out of the way. They were really the only two non-Montgomerys, and she could only imagine how they felt.

"The location is pretty damn perfect," Shep said with a grin. His wife Shea stood by his side, their daughter Livvy bouncing between them. How her niece had gotten so big, Adrienne had no idea. Apparently, time flew when you had your head down, working. "We're the only tattoo shop around here, which will be good for business." They were located in a strip mall off the busiest road in their area—other than I-25, of course. That's how most of the businesses around were set up, with only the large market chains and restaurants having actual acreage behind them.

Adrienne nodded, though her stomach didn't quite agree. Most of the shops like hers were farther south, near the older parts of downtown. There were trendier places there, and a lot more people who looked like they did with ink and piercings. Up north, on North Academy Blvd, every building was the same: cream or tan-colored, and fit in almost like a bedroom community around the Air Force Academy.

Shep and Adrienne wanted not only the cadets but also everyone who lived in the sprawling neighborhood who wanted ink to find them and come back for more. Beginning something new was always difficult, but starting something new in an area of town that, from the outside at least, didn't look as if they'd fit in wouldn't make it any easier.

She knew that a lot of the prejudices about tattoo shops had faded away over time as the art became far more popular and almost normal, but she could still feel people's eyes on her when they noticed her ink.

"It's right next to a tea shop, a deli, a spice shop, Thea's bakery, and a few fancy shopping areas. I think you fit in nicely," Austin said, his arms folded over his chest as he looked around the place. "You almost have a little version of what we have up north. You just need a bookstore and a café where you can hang out."

"You're just spoiled because you don't even have to walk outside into the cold to get coffee or baked goods," Adrienne said dryly.

"That is true," Austin said with a laugh. "Adding in

that side door that connects the two businesses was the best decision I ever made."

"I'll be sure to mention that to your wife," Shep said and ducked as Austin's arm shot out. The two men were nearly forty years old but fought like they were teens. Shea picked up Livvy and laughed before heading over to Maya. Adrienne didn't actually know her sister-in-law all that well since she hadn't seen her much, but now that the family had relocated, she knew that would change.

"They're going to break something," Thea said with a small laugh as she watched the two play-fight. She was the middle girl of the family but tended to act as if she were the eldest. When the retail spot three doors down from Thea's bakery had opened up, her sister had stopped at nothing to make sure Adrienne could move in. That was Thea, taking care of her family no matter what.

"Then they'll deserve it," Roxie, Adrienne's other sister said, shaking her head. "As long as they don't ruin something in the shop, of course," she added quickly after Adrienne shot her a look. "I meant break something on themselves." Roxie was the youngest of their immediate family, and often the quietest. None of them were truly quiet since they were Montgomerys, but Roxie sometimes fit the bill.

"Thanks for thinking of my shop that hasn't even had its first client yet." Adrienne wrapped her arm around Roxie's waist for a hug. "Where's Carter? I thought he said he'd be here."

Roxie and Carter had gotten married a few months ago, and Adrienne loved her brother-in-law, though she didn't know him all that well either. He worked long hours, and the couple tended to be very insular since they were still newlyweds.

Roxie's mouth twisted into a grimace before she schooled her features. "He couldn't get off work. He tried, but two guys called in, and he was up to his neck in carburetors."

Adrienne kissed her sister's temple and squeezed her tightly. "It's okay. It *is* the middle of the day, after all. I'm surprised any of you were able to take time off for this."

Tears formed at the backs of her eyes at the fact that everyone *had* taken the time to be there for her and Shep. She blinked. She looked up from her sisters and tried not to let her emotions get to her, but then she met Mace's eyes. He gave her a curious look, and she smiled at him, trying to let him know that she was okay —just a little overwhelmed. Mace had a way of knowing what she felt without her saying it, and she didn't want him to worry. That's what happened when you were friends with someone as long as they had been.

"I just wish he would have come," Roxie said with a shrug. "It's fine. Everything is fine."

Adrienne met Thea's gaze, but the two sisters didn't say anything. If Roxie had something she wanted to share, she would. For now, everyone had other things on their minds. Namely, opening day.

Shep punched Austin in the shoulder one more time before backing away and grinning. "Okay, okay, I'm too old for this shit."

"True, you *are* too old." Austin winked, and Adrienne pinched the bridge of her nose.

"Great way to show everyone that we're all *so* professional and ready to lead with our own shop," she said, no bite to her tone. This was her family, and she was used to it all. If they weren't joking around and being loveable, adorable dorks, she'd have thought something was wrong.

"It's sort of what we signed on for," Ryan said with a wink. "Right, Mace? I mean, the legendary Montgomery antics are why *any* tattoo artist worth their salt wants to join up with them."

Mace gave them all a solemn nod, laughter dancing in his eyes. "It wouldn't be a Montgomery gathering without someone getting punched. Isn't that what you taught me, Adrienne?"

She flipped him off, knowing that Livvy's head was down so she wouldn't see. She tried not to be *too* bad of an influence on her niece.

"Okay, party people. Finish your drinks and cake and then let's clean up. We have three clients scheduled between one and two this afternoon, and Ryan is handling any walk-ins." Though she wasn't sure there would *be* any walk-ins since it was day one and they were doing a slow start. Some of their long-time clients had moved with them, and they already had a waiting list because of it, but that could change on a dime. Having word of mouth would be what made their shop a success, and that meant getting more clients in who weren't just the same ones from before.

The door opened, and she held back her frown. They weren't officially open yet, but it wasn't as if she could tell a potential customer off. The door *had* been unlocked, after all.

As a man in a nicely cut suit with a frown on his face walked in, Adrienne had a feeling this wouldn't be a client.

"Hi there, can I help you?" she asked, moving her way through the crowd. "We're opening in an hour or so, but if you need any information, I'm here."

The guy's face pinched, and she was worried that if he kept it up, it would freeze like that. "I'm not here for whatever it is this establishment does." His gaze traveled over her family's and friend's ink and clothing before it rested back on her. "I'm only here to tell you that you shouldn't finish unpacking."

"Excuse me?" Shep asked, his tone serious. The others stood back, letting Adrienne and Shep talk, but she knew they were all there if she needed them.

"You heard me." The man adjusted his tie. "I don't know how you got through the zoning board, but I can see they made a mistake. We don't want *your kind* here in our nice city. We're a growing community with families. Like I said, don't unpack. You won't be here long."

Before she could say anything in response to the ridiculous statement, the man turned on his heel and walked out of her building, leaving her family and friends standing beside her, all of them with shocked looks on their faces.

"Well, shit," Mace whispered then winced as he looked behind him to where Livvy was most likely with her mom.

"We'll figure out who that was. But, Adrienne, he won't be able to shut us down or whatever the hell he wants." Shep turned to her and gave her that big-brother stare. "Don't stress about him. He means nothing."

But she could tell from the look in his eyes, and the worried glances passing back and forth between her family members and friends that none of them quite believed that.

She had no idea who the man was, but she had a bad feeling about him. And every single warm feeling that had filled her at the sight of her family and friends coming together to celebrate the new shop fled, replaced by ice water in her veins.

So much for an easy opening day, she thought, and her stomach roiled again. Perhaps she would throw up because she just knew that wasn't the last time they'd see that man. Not by a long shot.

CHAPTER TWO

Mace Knight really didn't want to wake up. His bed was far too warm, and he'd just had the most amazing dream featuring a fantasy woman with soft curves and a mouth that knew *exactly* what to do with his dick. Getting out of bed and having to shower and act like an adult didn't really match up to the dream woman and her seductive suction.

He sighed and gripped the base of his cock, annoyed with his morning wood that reminded him of his teenage self rather than a man of his age. But since he still had a few minutes, and he still had the image of the woman with her long, raven hair on her knees in front of him, he might as well enjoy his morning.

Sliding his hand up and down his shaft, he groaned

and planted his feet on his bed so he could thrust into his fist. He imagined her licking up his length before swallowing him whole. His eyes still closed, he sped up his pace, fucking his hand. It wasn't long before he came on his stomach, his body shaking with the release. He'd already been pretty damn close from his dream alone, so all it took was a few touches with as sensitive as he was in the mornings.

"Shit," he growled out as his heart rate settled back down. He let out a ragged breath. Now, he was not only running late, but he also had a sticky mess on his hand and stomach, and no way to clean it up since he didn't keep a box of tissues on his nightstand like any sane man should.

Annoyed with himself, he slid out of bed and hobbled his way to the bathroom, still holding his junk so he wouldn't make more of a mess. He should have just taken care of himself in the shower like usual since he was a single man with a healthy sexual appetite, but the dream woman had made him want to do something different that morning.

Looking down at himself in the mirror, he figured that next time he'd just take the dark-haired woman of his dreams into the shower with him, because now he had to change the damn sheets on his bed, too.

"Happy fucking morning," he grumbled and set

about getting ready for his day. He had two clients scheduled, and any walk-ins that showed up. Since they were only a crew of four, they rotated which days they each took off. Right now, Adrienne and Ryan worked most of the weekends since they'd all decided that Shep needed some time with his family, especially right after the move. Shep would cycle in and out of the weekend shift since it was their busiest time, and he didn't want to slack off, or so he'd said. Mace only took off on the weekends he had Daisy, his four-year-old daughter, who he only had partial custody of. He didn't see her often enough as it was, and while it had been a pain in the ass at his old place to get time off for her, everyone was bending over backwards for him now.

He had a good feeling about this place, and he was so damned happy that he'd taken the risk to move to a new shop. Yeah, the guy who had come in and made the vague threat last week on opening day worried him, but Mace knew he'd put his trust in his best friend and her family for a reason. Getting more family time with his little girl was only part of that.

After he'd gotten dressed for the day and went to make himself some coffee, he pulled out his phone to text Adrienne. Since they were on the same shift most days—even at the old place—and lived close to each other, they tried to carpool as much as possible. The strip mall where the new shop was located had decent parking, but on busy days when the other stores and eateries were packed, they wanted to take up less space.

Mace: *You up?*

He sipped his coffee as the little bubble on her end of the conversation popped up.

Addi: *Yes, but I need more coffee. All the coffee. Ever.*

Mace grinned and paged through his notebook, glancing at his sketches for his first client. The cadet wanted a set of twisted trees on one shoulder to signify an event from his past with his family. He wouldn't explain to Mace exactly what it was, but he had given enough detail for Mace to get the idea down for him. He'd also had to relearn all the rules and regulations regarding tattoos that came with being a part of any military branch. Things had changed so much in the past ten years that it almost took a math degree to figure out percentages of skin and placements. With the amount of ink covering Mace's chest, arms, and back, there was no way he'd ever be able to join up—not that it had ever been in the cards for him, even since the beginning.

Mace: *You still want a ride to work? Or you going in early?*

Addi: *Let's save the environment.*

Mace snorted before draining the last of his coffee.

He'd need another cup before he headed over to Adrienne's to pick her up. Hell, he might need a third cup, considering he hadn't slept well the night before.

Mace: *Pick you up in an hour.*

Addi: *kk.*

Mace: *What's with the two ks?*

Addi: *...*

Addi: *Are you really asking me about texting lingo when I've only had half a cup of coffee after being up all night? And I have no idea, Austin's kid starting doing it, and then Austin assimilated it, and now I'm doing it. Apparently, it's hip with the cool kids.*

Mace had to set his second cup of coffee down on the counter so he wouldn't slosh the hot liquid over the sides. He had no idea how she'd texted so fast, but she could probably beat some of those so-called *cool kids* at the texting game. He and Adrienne had been forced to learn texting by tapping numbers more than once for different letters back in the age-old times of the first popular cell phones.

And now he felt old at the ripe age of thirty-five. He needed more coffee for that line of thought.

Mace: *If you're using the lingo, the kids don't use it anymore, just saying.*

He frowned and texted her again before she could curse at him.

Mace: *And what were you up doing all night? You catch his name?*

He had no idea why he'd asked that or why it was even his business, but for some reason, he'd let his mind wander a little too much.

Addi: *I was working on a damn sketch, dumbass. The other probably would have been more fun since I got stuck in my head for three hours before I finally figured the design out. Now, for real, gotta shower. Go clean that beard of yours, old man.*

He flipped her off in an emoji, then set his phone down so he could finish his morning routine. He was just finishing cleaning up when the doorbell rang. He frowned, wondering who could be at his house that early in the morning since most of his friends were either already at work or worked nights and were probably just waking up like he was.

Stuffing his phone into his pocket, he made his way to the front door and blinked when he saw his ex through the peephole. Then he held back a curse when he noticed that she wasn't alone.

He threw open the door but kept his anger in check because, beside Jeaniene in her pressed suit and to-the-nines makeup and hair, was their little girl, Daisy. He raised a questioning brow at his ex then went to his knees and opened his arms. Without hesitation, Daisy jumped into his hold, and he picked her up, holding her hard to his chest. She kissed his temple, then his forehead, then his cheek, before sighing and resting her head on his shoulder.

That wasn't unusual for her since she wasn't the most talkative kid. She only said things when they seemed important to her. She was sweet as could be and whisper-giggled to her imaginary fairy friends more often than not, but she was really shy when it came to the real world. He didn't care as long as she was happy and he got to see her—but that wasn't often with the custody agreement in place. Jeaniene got full custody, while he only had visitation. That's what happened when one parent was a lawyer in a family of lawyers, and the other was a tattoo artist without a college degree. He'd fought with all his savings but had won visitation only.

This wasn't his weekend, though; yet Daisy's suitcase was on the step behind his ex.

"What's up, Jeaniene?" He rubbed Daisy's back as she clung to him.

"Hi, Daddy," she said sleepily.

"Hi, baby." He kissed the top of her head. "You okay?"

"Uh-huh, just sleepy." She snuggled into his

shoulder and started playing with his hair, her mind in her little dream world. "Jeaniene?"

She gestured behind him. "Can we go inside for a second? I don't have a lot of time and, honestly, I didn't know how to say this on the phone. I *know* I'm doing this horribly, but…just…can you give me a moment, Mace?"

He studied her face and knew that he wouldn't like whatever she had to say, but as he had his daughter in his arms, it wasn't like he had much of a choice. Jeaniene followed behind, rolling Daisy's suitcase behind her. His ex seemed nervous, which was very unlike her, but he didn't press. Not yet, and not with Daisy snuggled against him.

He and Jeaniene had only been together a few times, and just for fun with no real ties, when she found out she was pregnant. Everything had gone to shit after that, but in the end, he'd gotten his baby girl, so he counted it as one hell of a win.

Mace set Daisy down on the couch and kissed the top of her head before handing her his phone. Wasn't the best parenting, but he needed to talk to Jeaniene in private, and he didn't want Daisy to overhear. "Be right back, pumpkin." He quickly opened up the child memory app game that he knew she liked, ran a hand over her hair, then gestured for Jeaniene to follow him into the kitchen.

"What's going on, Jeaniene?" His coffee sat like lead in his gut, and he knew he'd probably regret that second cup.

She bit her lip, an action very unlike her, and he tilted his head, studying her face. She looked as if she hadn't slept much the night before, something she couldn't hide even with all her professional attire and makeup. If something was worrying her that much, he knew he wouldn't like it.

"I got partner," she said quickly, and his brows rose.

"Really? Good for you." And he meant it. She worked her ass off at her job *and* still made time for Daisy. He could never fault her for how she cared for their daughter, even if he wanted to rail at her for not letting him be in Daisy's life enough for his liking. "You did that pretty quick, right?" She was far younger than the men at her firm—younger than even Mace—so her making partner was actually a big thing.

She nodded but didn't look any less stressed. "Actually, that's not completely accurate. I *will* make partner this month. If I do something."

He stiffened. "And what the hell do you need to do?" Hypothetical situations raced through his head that would put her in a compromising position, and he curled his fists. He knew what kind of men she worked with and the power they wielded. He might not like Jeaniene as much as he had when they were together, but if someone hurt her, he'd have to do something about it.

She raised her hands, palms facing him, and shook her head. "Nothing like what you're thinking. I promise. But it's still bad."

"Spit it out, Jeaniene."

"I'll make partner if I move to Japan. Tomorrow. No warning, no preparation. But a spot opened up, and the *only* way I'll make partner before I'm forty at this firm is if I do this. It's a great opportunity, and will set up Daisy and me for the rest of our lives if I go along with this new position for six months."

His mouth went dry as his brain tried to catch up. Japan, for six months? What. The. Fuck.

He hadn't realized he'd said it aloud until her brows rose pointedly and she glared in his direction. She'd never liked his cursing, but she could fuck right off just then.

"You're moving to Japan? What about Daisy? There's no fucking way you're taking her out of the damn country. She's my daughter, too, damn it."

A pained look crossed her face, and she let out a breath. "I can't bring Daisy with me, Mace." She whispered it as if she couldn't quite believe the words coming out of her mouth either.

"What?" he asked, his voice hoarse. He couldn't have heard her right. There was no way she was just dropping their daughter off at his house with no warning or discussion. He did his best to ignore the suitcase she'd brought with her.

"It will be best if Daisy stays here in the US. I'll be working long hours in Japan, and frankly, I don't know how I'll be able to be a full-time mom over there."

He just blinked, confused as all hell and ignoring that little kernel of hope in his heart that he might be seeing Daisy more than before. Because this was Jeaniene, after all, and nothing was ever as it seemed.

"My parents offered to take Daisy in, of course."

"No fucking way. She's *my* daughter. Not theirs." Something Jeaniene's family tended to forget. "If you're going to leave Daisy and go gallivanting off across the world, putting work before your child, then you're damn well going to make sure she's with her *father*."

Anger sparked in her eyes, but she didn't curse at him. Jeaniene wouldn't. "I wasn't going to let them take her. Despite what they say, you *are* a good father. And it's going to kill me to leave her here with only Skype and some visits if I can get those planned, but it will be the best for us in the end if I make partner. I'm doing this for her."

He didn't believe that for even a hot second, but he wasn't sure he had words for what he was feeling right then.

Jeaniene looked down at her watch and then pressed her lips together into a tight line. "I don't know all the details, and this will have to be done legally, of course. The firm will send you papers on what the temporary situation is, and then the two of us can decide what the permanent solution will be. I need to go if I'm going to make my flight." Tears pooled in her eyes, but he ignored them. "Mace. I need you to watch Daisy until I can figure out what to do. This will be good for our future, I know it, but...but I also know this puts a lot of responsibility on your shoulders. If it's too much, I can talk to my parents."

He held up his hand, his chest heaving. He honestly couldn't fucking believe what was going on. Jeaniene had done a lot of things that not only surprised him but had also pissed him off throughout the years, but this... this topped anything he could have ever even dreamed of.

"Let me get this straight. You're moving to Japan. Now. No warning. No phone call to tell me what the fuck you're planning. And you're leaving Daisy here.

Again, no warning. Don't get me wrong, it's not that I don't want her to live here. Not that I don't want her with me. Always. It's the fact that you don't seem to fucking care that you're abandoning your kid. But...you do you. Like you always do. But that paperwork you're sending? You can be damn sure I'll get a better lawyer than I had last time. And you'd better have something in writing *now* before you go so your parents don't try to pull some shit, or I'm going to make your life hell. You get me?"

She raised her chin and met his gaze. "I get you, Mace. I always *got* you." She reached into her purse and pulled out a stack of papers. "I got these done already. It will cover you from my family. We'll deal with the rest soon. And as for Daisy? I'm doing this *for* her."

"Whatever you need to tell yourself at night."

She shot him a look and stalked back into the living room where he guessed she was saying goodbye to their daughter. Mace let out a shuddering breath then gripped the edge of the counter, trying to figure out what the hell had just happened.

From one breath to the next, he'd become a full-time dad.

And he had no idea what the fuck to do about it.

CHAPTER THREE

It had been a week since Adrienne watched her best friend's life change dramatically, and she still wasn't sure either of them had found their footing. She still couldn't quite believe that Jeaniene had left the country as quickly as she had, leaving behind not only most of her belongings to be packed and either stored or shipped later but also her *daughter*.

What kind of mother did that?

Sure, Mace had said the woman mentioned over and over again that it was for Daisy's future, but that didn't sit well with Adrienne, and she wasn't sure if she would be able to hold back laying into the woman if she ever saw her again. It wasn't as if the two of them had been great friends when Jeaniene and Mace were together. The other woman had always been slightly jealous of Adrienne's relationship with Mace, even though there was nothing more than platonic friendship between them. And Adrienne had hated the fact that there was tension because of something so silly and superficial. But it wasn't as if Mace and Jeaniene had been serious—at least until Daisy came along. Then everything had imploded, and Adrienne had just done her best to stand by her best friend's side and hold him up when things went from bad to worse.

Maybe if Adrienne had gotten to know Mace's ex, she'd have liked her more, but from what she'd seen, she really had no evidence to support that probability. And that just sucked for everyone involved—most especially Daisy.

Now, it had been a week since Jeaniene left Daisy with Mace, and her best friend had been forced to figure out how to be a full-time dad without any notice or preparation, along with holding down a full-time job. Sure, Daisy had a room at his place and clothes and toys and things, but they had a rhythm for their *weekends* together, not anything close to what they needed now.

Thankfully, Mace lived in the same school district as Daisy's former home; he'd made sure of that when he moved to his new place a couple of years ago. He hadn't wanted to disrupt Daisy's life at all, and there was no way Jeaniene would have moved for him. But it meant that Mace had moved even closer to Adrienne in the process, and she hadn't minded one bit.

It also meant that Daisy didn't have to change preschools and could stay with her friends when she moved into kindergarten and beyond. Unless everything changed dramatically again. But then they'd just have to come up with a new plan.

While Mace and his parents were holding most of the baggage, Adrienne was doing her best to help, as well. The Knights watched Daisy during the day when Mace needed to work, and the girl wasn't in her half-days of school. Mace needed the hours, and Adrienne needed him working as well since they'd just started the business. But Ryan and Shep had agreed to allow Mace to have whatever hours he needed for the time being. And in the evenings, when she wasn't working, Adrienne headed over to Mace's place and made sure they had a good meal on the table. It wasn't that she was a better cook than Mace—in fact, she thought he was far better—but she'd known that figuring out the timing of meals, bath time, and when to go to bed in the middle of the week, all while trying to keep from making anything too straining on a little girl wouldn't be easy.

So she did what she could to help, and tried her best to stay out of the way. She loved Daisy and would do anything to make sure Mace could be the best dad he could be. And if that meant stressing out over things out of her control like usual, well, that was something she was just going to have to do.

"You're woolgathering in the corner over there again," Mace said, startling her.

She hadn't realized he was back from picking up food for them over at the deli a couple of doors down. They used to bring in their lunch every day at their old job since finances were always an issue, but since they'd all been a little too busy thinking about anything except work and Daisy lately, things like packing up lunches had gone to the wayside far too easily.

She turned to see Mace holding out a bottle of water and her wrapped sandwich, and she let out a breath. "You scared the crap out of me."

He raised a brow. "If I had, you'd have screamed like you did that one time we went to that corn maze."

She glared but didn't take her food since she didn't want it in her booth. "I did not scream that loudly. And if I *had,* no one would have blamed me. There was a *clown.* With a *chainsaw. Chasing* me."

Mace just grinned and leaned against the half-wall that made up her booth. "I've never actually seen you run that quickly or jump that high over that hole in the ground that was supposed to slow you down. It was like you were doing hurdles or something."

"Clown. Chainsaw. Chasing." She held up her hand, pointing up her fingers as she ticked off her list. "The three C's of doom."

"I'm sure there are other C's out there that could make it better."

And for some reason, the way his voice growled just that certain way he did to make her laugh, she blushed. Her cheeks heated to the point where she knew he probably saw it but, hopefully, he'd think it was anger. She was *not* going to be embarrassed—or worse, turned on—because of the man in front of her.

There were lines she didn't cross, and that was one of them.

And, recently, she'd had to be extra cautious what direction her thoughts traveled when it came to Mace. Apparently, opening up her own business while dealing with a slew of other things had made her lose sight of what was important.

"Whatever you say, Knight." She swallowed hard and moved back a bit so she could have some breathing room. Mace was just so *big* that he ended up taking up more space than anyone else she knew. And considering how big her brothers and cousins were, that was saying something.

He winked and went back to the side table where he'd left his sandwich. Ryan was at his station working and would close up once Adrienne and Mace left, and neither of them wanted to bother the man since he was focusing. Sure, all of them were good at working while the place was busy, but she'd let him work in peace if she could.

She and Mace dug into their food while keeping an eye out for any walk-ins. Since it was the middle of the week and raining, she didn't think they'd get any, but she had to stay vigilant. It had been a full day of family already. Shep was home for the evening with his family, and Shea had already been by with Roxie since the two of them were the shop's accountants. Soon, Adrienne and Mace would head home and leave Ryan to handle any last-minute things, but she trusted the man. After all, she couldn't open and close *every* day.

Just most days it seemed since she was the one without connections or anyone to come home to after a long day of work and stress. That hadn't bothered her before as she'd always been focused on her dreams and might have kept an eye out for a man who could be *the one*, but it hadn't been a priority. Now, though, for some reason, things weren't like they had been before. Maybe because she'd accomplished her dream of owning a shop, and even though she had to work even harder to maintain it, that part of her checklist was done? Not to mention the fact that Shep was back in town with his perfect family, and Roxie was already married. She hadn't felt left behind before, but the more she thought about it now, the more those creeping feelings kept coming back.

Mace had Daisy at home now, and Thea...well, Thea was a workaholic at her bakery much like Adrienne was at the shop, so maybe the two of them were their own peas in a pod.

"Again with the woolgathering," Mace said, brushing his shoulder against hers as they sat on the couch in the front of the shop.

"What does woolgathering even mean?" she asked, quickly pushing her earlier odd thoughts from her mind.

Mace frowned. "You know, I don't really know, and that makes me feel like kind of an idiot." He pulled out his phone and started scrolling. "Let's look it up."

She rolled her eyes and couldn't help but smile as he looked up the definition and taught them something new for the day. Well, at least she'd never be bored with him by her side.

"That man come back?" Mace said after they'd cleaned up and started working on cleaning the rest of the place.

She shook her head, knowing exactly whom he meant. "No, but I don't think that one time will be the last time we hear from him. Shep's been looking into who he could be, but honestly, it's a dead end right now. He didn't introduce himself. He just threatened us with weird, vague shit." It still didn't feel right to her, and she *knew* there would be more from that visit soon. She just hated the fact that it was a waiting game until they figured it out.

"I don't want you alone here at night, Adrienne. Not when we don't know what that man's issue was other than being a stuck-up suit with a sneering problem."

That made her pause, her hands fisting in front of her on the counter. "Excuse me? Did you tell Shep or Ryan that you don't want *them* alone?"

Ryan's client had just left, so he looked up from his notebook before holding up his hands in surrender. "No, he didn't, and for the love of God, keep me out of it."

Mace flipped him off, but Adrienne could only glare at her so-called best friend. "Addi."

"Don't fucking *Addi* me. I know you're overprotective, but remember, I can take care of myself. Plus, this is a brightly lit area, and even if I'm the last one out of the shop, it's not like I didn't do that for years at the old place. Don't get all dude bro on me, Mace. I'm not going to take kindly to that."

Ryan snorted. "Dude bro?"

She flipped him off since he could be just like Mace and Shep and go all overprotective if they thought one of their *women* was in danger. Not that Adrienne had ever been in danger when she walked into the parking lot. Like any sane woman walking alone at night, she walked to her car with either her pepper spray in her hand or her keys in her fist. Of course, when she told Mace that, he just glowered harder.

Men.

"I'm just saying…"

"Don't say anything. I'm not going to wait for a strong man to save me just so I can walk outside, but I'm also not going to be stupid. I know there are people out there who like to prey on women. Hello? I'm a woman, and the fact that I walk to my car like I do and I've never been attacked should tell you something. But I'm also not going to live my life afraid of what *might* happen and end up hurting the business and create issues with everyone else's hours because of it."

Mace sighed before leaning against the wall. "I get it. And I know I shouldn't have even said anything, but that dude creeped me out, and frankly, I don't trust what he might do."

Her stomach twisted, but she ignored it. "That man is more likely to sue us for some petty shit we didn't do, Mace. That is what we should be worrying about." The idea of just that kept her up late at night—not that she said as much to Mace and Ryan.

"Okay, you two, there's nothing you can do about it now," Ryan said, coming between the two of them. "You're both off the clock anyway, and since you're leaving at the same time, Mace can get all protective and walk you to your car, Adrienne, and you can glare the whole time, knowing that you're not changing up your schedule so he can do it."

"I'm starting to wonder why we hired you," Adrienne said with a growl before going back to pick up her things. The rain had picked up, and it was freaking cold outside, so she needed her coat.

"Because I'm God's gift to tattooing, and I take your ribbing easily."

Mace was the one to laugh aloud at that, and Adrienne couldn't help but smile. "Whatever you say, Ryan. Whatever you say."

Mace went to pick up his things as well, and soon, the two of them were walking side by side in the pouring rain out to their cars. They'd parked far away, so she was drenched by the time she got to her door.

Their vehicles were next to each other as usual, and she gave him a mock salute as she slid into the driver's seat.

He grinned and got into his truck, shaking his head the whole time. Yeah, they fought, but they were best friends for a reason. She understood why he worried about her and knew she would be even more vigilant when she walked alone, but there was no way she was going to change everyone's hours to suit the whims of the overprotective.

She turned her key in the ignition and then cursed as it just clicked. No trying to turn over, no weird sounds, just a click.

"What the fuck?" She tried again, taking deep breaths so she wouldn't lose her temper and start beating the shit out of her steering wheel. The only thing that would end up broken would be her hand—and whatever was already screwed up under the hood.

"Damn it!" she yelled again as it continued to click with no results.

Someone tapped on her window, and she screamed much like she had in that corn maze, even though she knew it had to be Mace being all overprotective again.

She opened her door after letting out a long sigh, then grabbed her bag and made sure Mace was out of the way before standing up.

"If you ask to check under the hood before I get a chance to, I might knee you in the balls."

Rain poured down on them, and he just shook his head. "It's probably the battery, right?"

"What did I say about the hood? No guessing. No trying to fix the problem until I can see what's going on."

"Come on, Addi, it's fucking pouring, and you're on the way home anyway. Let's just leave your car here instead of dealing with whatever is wrong with it when neither of us has any skill whatsoever when it comes to engines. We'll call Roxie's husband to come and take a look at it tomorrow, and I'll give you a ride to work in the morning."

Roxie's husband, Carter, *was* a mechanic, and even if it was just the battery—though she wasn't sure since she knew nothing about cars—the weather sucked enough that she'd end up electrocuting herself rather than jumping her vehicle.

"Fine." Rain slid down her neck and in between her breasts, her coat doing nothing against the October chill or the precipitation. She knew she'd sounded petulant, but she was so tired of her damn car and its issues. She needed a new one, badly, but she'd used most of her savings for her house and the shop. Sure, she had some left, but she knew she needed to keep a bit for a rainy day—pun unintended. Mace shut her door behind her before turning to open his passenger side door for her. She sighed, hugged him quickly because she felt like a brat, then climbed up into his truck.

When he ran around to the driver's side and hopped in, she rested her head back on the headrest and let out a sigh.

"I'm sorry I'm grumpy. Thank you for driving me home and helping me deal with my car. I know it's raining and yucky and you're being amazing. I'm just growly."

Mace reached over and squeezed her hand before turning the ignition and pulling out of the spot. "You're not grumpy or growly. Not really," he added when she snorted. "Your car wouldn't start, and you didn't kick the tire or anything, so that's progress."

She couldn't help the smile that spread across her face as she looked over at him. "I kicked my tire *once*, and that was because I was annoyed with Joe."

"Your ex was a douche, so you should have kicked *his* tire instead of yours, but then that would have been a misdemeanor."

Mace wasn't wrong that Joe was a douche, but she hadn't even seen the other man in over a year. She blinked, her mouth going dry.

Over. A. Year.

"Oh my God," she whispered. If she hadn't seen the man in over year, that meant she hadn't had sex in over a year. Over three hundred and sixty-five days of only having an orgasm because she knew how to rub her clit and had a very nice bag full of toys.

Oh. Dear. God.

Mace turned to her sharply before looking back at the road. "What is it? Shit, I thought I was going to hit something."

She winced. "Sorry. At least you didn't swerve."

"What's wrong? You're pale and look like you're going to be sick. Do I need to pull over?" He started looking to the side, and she reached out and patted his arm.

"I'm fine. Really. I uh…just thought about something alarming and, well, it surprised me, that's all."

He kept his eyes on the road as the rain started coming down harder, but she saw the confusion on his face. She usually told him what she was thinking, but she wasn't sure she was ready to tell him this.

Ever.

They sat in awkward silence as Mace made his way to her house, and she tried to figure out how she'd let her dating and sex lives lapse as they had. She'd been busy working on setting up the new shop and working double-time at her old place to save up before she quit, so that was an easy excuse.

Still, though, she wasn't quite sure how it had happened.

Mace pulled into her driveway, and the rain around them came down in sheets, the wind slamming into his truck hard enough to rock it on its wheels.

"You can't drive in this," she said over the roaring wind. "It should die down soon, but at least come inside for a bit while you wait. You know how this area floods. Your parents have Daisy, right?"

Mace turned off the engine and nodded. "Yeah, they're at my house since we don't have our system down yet."

"Then come on in for a bit and wait for the wind to at least die down."

The truck rocked again.

"Sounds like a plan," he said as he met her gaze. Then, they were both running through the wind and rain, laughing as she tried to get her key into the lock. They tumbled into her house together, his hands on her upper arms, keeping her steady as they slid across the hardwood floor and slammed the door behind them.

"That was crazy!" she laughed, shaking her head, watching the water drops fall from her hair as if she'd just gotten out of the shower.

He squeezed her arms, letting her go, and a chill slid over her. She assumed it had to be from the wet rain that was slowly turning to ice outside.

"Came out of nowhere. Hopefully, Ryan's okay at the shop."

"He should be fine. I mean, these storms never last for long. Not without snow anyway. Want a towel?"

He nodded and followed her back to the master bath. She handed him a fluffy bath sheet then took one for herself. "So, you going to tell me what you were thinking about?"

She froze. "Uh…"

"Just tell me. You got me all curious." He ran his towel through his hair, and she couldn't help but watch the way the muscles in his arms bunched at the movement. Her best friend was damn sexy and, apparently, she needed to get laid because she couldn't keep her mind off him.

Nothing good could come from what she was going to say next, nor the directions of her thoughts but, apparently, the cold had rattled her brain.

"I was thinking that I haven't had sex in over a year." She paused, but he just looked at her, his eyes wide. "And that it's been so long, that you're looking really hot all wet and bearded."

He didn't say anything, his gaze on hers. She was

really afraid she'd just fucked everything up. All she had to do was laugh it off and make it a joke. Tell him that she was just kidding and wanted to make him squirm.

But she didn't say anything.

Couldn't say anything.

And he didn't say anything either.

Instead, he tilted his head, making her feel like she'd ruined everything.

And then he kissed her.

Hard.

CHAPTER FOUR

Mace was making a fucking mistake, and he didn't care. Adrienne tasted like sin and seduction, and he knew if he stopped kissing her, he'd let his mind wander to what the hell he was doing, and he'd fuck up everything even more.

So, he kept kissing her.

And then he took it deeper.

His fingers tangled in her hair, and she slid her hands up his chest, digging into his flesh. Their moans were lost in the wind and rain outside as it beat down on the bathroom window, and he couldn't help but explore her mouth.

He'd thought about doing this countless times; thought about tasting her, having her. He'd imagined himself licking up her neck and down between her breasts before devouring her everywhere else. He'd thought about how she'd arch into him as he plunged into her, and they'd both come, panting and sweaty.

He'd thought about all of it because he'd been attracted to Addi from day one, but had never wanted to hurt their friendship. That was still the case because she was the most important adult in his life, the strongest relationship he had with another person besides Daisy.

So why was he still kissing her?

Mace was about to pull back when she leaned in closer, her breasts pressing into his chest. And when her hands slid around to his back to cling to him, he knew there would be no getting out of this mistake just then.

They'd deal with the consequences later because that's what they did. They were strong enough to deal with anything, and right then, all he wanted to do was bury himself inside his best friend and never stop.

So, he didn't.

He licked and nibbled up her jaw, loving the way she arched her neck for him in response. He couldn't reach all of her shoulder, and he wanted nothing more than to taste every inch of her skin, so he pulled back and tugged on the bottom of her shirt. She blinked up at him with wide, lust-filled eyes then helped him strip the garment over her head.

That still left her in a tank, where he could just barely glimpse some delicate lace that made his mouth water.

"Why the fuck are you wearing so many clothes?"

"Because if I wear this bra under just a cotton shirt, you can see all the bumps from the lace, and I'm really not in the mood to deal with dude bros trying to wonder what the hell is all over my tits."

He shook his head and pulled her tank off quickly before leaning down and sucking one lace-covered nipple into his mouth. Her head fell back, and she moaned, her hand in his hair, pressing him closer to her.

"Now I'm the one all over your tits," he teased then moved to her other breast.

She gave a laugh that ended on a groan as he slid her bra down slightly so he could bare her breast.

"That was hor—" A lust-filled gasp. "A horrible joke. Like the worst, ever."

"Then let me make it up to you." He sucked on her other breast, reaching around her back to undo her bra clasp with one hand.

"Take off your shirt. That could help."

He grinned, leaning back to do as she asked. Well,

demanded, but he didn't mind just then, especially if she ordered him around like that. As long as they were about to be skin-to-skin, he'd do whatever she wanted.

"I freaking love your ink," she whispered. "Like, I know that I got to do the work on your legs, but your old artist who did *all* of the ink on your chest and arms? Fucking talented."

His entire chest and arms were covered with an array of ink that was not only interconnected, but each meant something to him in a different and personal way. His artist had done it over a period of ten years at his old shop before he moved away. Adrienne had then taken over his ink, and since his entire back was tattoo-free, he knew she was ready to play with that canvas.

But not right then.

He kissed her again before going back to give more attention to her breasts. "You know you can have my back when we finish the design."

"You'll be *on* your back soon, Knight, so just keep that in mind."

He straightened then crushed his mouth to hers. "I think you've got that the other way around." He slid his hands down over the soft curve of her hips, then moved one around to her belly before dipping beneath the waistband of her jeans.

Her eyes met his as his fingers slid into her panties and then over the heat of her. "Mace."

He gently flicked his finger over her clit—a feat not easily done as her jeans were fucking tight, but the limited room to work gave them both a sense of urgency he knew would keep them on the edge.

"You're already so wet for me, Addi. Your panties are fucking damp, and I'm just now putting my fingers in your pussy." He pumped one finger in and out of her, just a bare graze as he couldn't move as much as he wanted, and watched as her pupils dilated and her breaths came in pants. "You going to be a good girl and come on my hand with your pants still on? You do that, and I'll lick this wet pussy of yours. I'll lick and suck, and eat you out until you come on my face. Then I'll fuck you hard until you break over my cock and leave scratches on my back. What do you say?" He entered a second finger, and her tight cunt pulsated around him. "You think you can do that? Can you come on my hand?"

They were standing in her bathroom with the rain slamming into the window, yet all he could do was move his fingers in and out of her with shallow, desperate strokes as she watched him with wide eyes.

"Addi? Can you come?"

In answer, she cupped her breasts and arched into him, her gaze never leaving his.

Then she came.

He'd known she was beautiful, had seen it every damn day, but he hadn't known the wonder and breathtaking radiance that was Addi when she came.

Her pussy clamped down on his fingers, and a stunning blush spread across her skin. "Mace."

At the sound of his name on her lips, he kissed her again, his fingers still moving in and out of her slick sheath. She was so wet, and the sounds they made together caused his cock to harden beyond reason. He was actually worried he might come in his jeans like a damn teenager, and if he weren't careful, he wouldn't be able to fuck her hard like he wanted.

So, he pulled his fingers out of her, looked right into her eyes, and licked her sweetness from the two fingers that had made her come like a fucking goddess.

"Jesus Christ, that's like the sexiest thing I've ever seen."

He winked. "You haven't seen my cock yet."

When she rolled her eyes, he couldn't help but grin. "Ego much?"

"Made you come with just my fingers, didn't I?"

"Yeah, yeah, yeah. Now put your mouth where your fingers were, and then we'll see."

There was a reason this woman was his best friend, and that mouth of hers was just part of it. He kissed her again, this time going slow so he could savor their time together because he had a feeling once they both left this haze of sex and bad decisions, they'd never touch each other like this again.

When he pulled way, he quickly pulled her jeans down along with her panties. Any other time, he'd have loved to use that lacy excuse for panties to play with her ass and her clit, but he didn't have the patience for that. She let out a surprised squeal when he lifted her up by the hips and set her down on the bathroom counter. Then, he pulled her to the edge, spread her legs, and licked her pussy in one quick set of movements, just to watch the way her body tightened.

"You're going to make me fall off this damn thing," she warned. "This isn't the sturdiest of counters."

"Then hold on," he growled and went back to eating her out. He licked between her folds, his hands holding down her thighs so he could spread her open and spear her with his tongue. She kept her hands on the edge of the counter so she wouldn't fall, but he knew it was damn close because her whole body shook as he licked and sucked and ate.

When her breaths came in tiny pants and her thighs

shook under his hands, he sucked on her clit again and looked up her body to her face.

"Mace."

And then she came again. He lapped her up, aware that if he didn't get inside her soon, he'd burst right then and there. He stood up quickly and undid his pants, thankful that they'd both taken off their shoes at the door since they were drenched. When he stood between her spread legs and wrapped her hair around his fist, she smiled up at him, the look in her eyes one of a woman drunk on lust, and he knew his likely mirrored hers even though he hadn't come yet. He crushed his mouth to hers, his need for her intensifying to the point where he wasn't sure he'd ever come back from it, at least not whole.

"Spare condoms are in the drawer," she panted, her legs wrapped around his waist, her pussy wet and hot against his stomach. He was damn glad she'd remembered a condom because she was so fucking sexy right then, he'd almost fucked her bare, and that wasn't something either of them was ready for. Hell, he wasn't sure that was something they'd *ever* be ready for.

"Spare?" he asked, fumbling for the drawer beside them. He quickly found the box of condoms, ripped open the container, then did the same to the packet before sliding the rubber over his length.

"I have more in the bedroom. These are in here in case I run out in there. I mean, it's not like I want to run from the bedroom to the bathroom for a condom, you know? Breaks the mood."

He *really* didn't want to think about another man fucking her at the moment, so he pushed those images from his head. "Thankfully, I'm going to fuck you right on this counter, so that works." He kissed her hard then pulled back so he could look into her eyes as he slid into her, inch by aching inch until he was seated to the hilt inside her wet heat.

"You're so fucking big," she whispered, laughter dancing in her eyes. "And I can't believe I just said that out loud."

He grinned, pumping his hips slightly so he moved in and out of her. "Well, a guy needs those kinds of compliments. And you're really tight. Perfect combination."

She lifted her hips slightly from the counter, bringing him deeper, and they both moaned.

"Fuuuuuck," he growled. "Hold on tight, Addi."

"As long as you make me come, I can do that."

He kissed her again. "Done."

Then he *moved*.

He had one hand on her hip, holding her so tightly

to him that he knew he'd probably leave a bruise. The other was on the back of her neck so they had their heads together, their gazes down, watching his length move in and out of her. It was singularly the most erotic sight he'd ever witnessed, and as his balls grew tight, he knew if he didn't make her come fast, she'd make a liar out of him with her sweet pussy.

Mace kissed her again then moved his hand from the back of her head to play with her clit. "Come, Addi. Come on my cock."

"Demanding."

He flicked her clit. "Needy."

"Fuck, yeah," she whispered and then broke apart as she came again. Her cunt was like a vice on his dick, and he came with her, swallowing her scream with his kiss as he thrust in and out of her with frenzied need on the wave of their orgasms.

Soon the sound of their breathing was the only noise in the bathroom, and he looked at the window, noticing that the rain had all but died down, and the wind was no longer making the house rattle.

Then, the reality of the situation hit him.

He was late picking up his daughter because he'd spent the past thirty minutes fucking his best friend in her bathroom. He still had his damn cock inside her, and neither of them had said anything since they both came so hard he was pretty sure he'd see stars for the next hour.

They'd made a huge fucking mistake, and as he looked into her eyes, he knew she knew it, too. But instead of kissing her like he should and telling her everything would be okay, he pulled out of her and disposed of the condom. How could everything be okay when neither of them had spoken a word to each other about what they were doing? This...need for each other might have always been there, but their acting on it had come out of nowhere.

"I have to go pick up Daisy."

Adrienne blinked and then closed her legs, covering up her breasts as much as she could with one arm as she nodded. He was a fucking bastard, but he had no idea what he should say to make everything okay.

He was ruining his best relationships because he was so far out of his depth, yet he had no idea how to fix it.

"Go, she's probably wondering where you are." There was no censure in her tone, no hurt, but the lack of emotion spoke volumes.

"I'll pick you up in the morning?" he asked, pulling up his jeans. "Are you going to call Carter tonight."

She nodded, her hands still covering herself, though

he'd tasted every inch she now hid from his sight. "I'll get it done." She cleared her throat. "Uh, see you tomorrow."

He met her gaze, willing either himself or her to say something, to say *anything* to make this better. But they hadn't said a word before they did what they'd done, and with so many emotions running high, he knew they wouldn't now either.

Not yet.

"Okay, then."

"Okay. Bye, Mace."

He swallowed hard. "Bye, Addi."

Then he left his best friend sitting on her bathroom counter, naked in more ways than one, as he went to pull on his shirt and shoes before walking out of her house and hoping to hell and back that he hadn't just fucked up their relationship for good.

The next morning wasn't awkward.

It was *fucking* awkward.

After he'd left Adrienne in her house without talking about what was important because God forbid they actually *talk* about what had just happened, he'd headed to his parent's house to pick up Daisy. His folks hadn't said a thing about his being late

—neither had Daisy for that matter—and he supposed they all assumed it had to do with the weather. Indirectly it had, sure, but he was seriously going to Hell for the decisions he'd made that day.

He'd tossed and turned all night, unable to get the taste and feel of his best friend from his mind. He'd almost texted her countless times but had no idea what to say to her. He didn't regret what he'd felt when he was with her, but he damn sure regretted how he'd made her feel when he left. They should have talked, should have made a thoughtful decision instead of doing something that could possibly ruin their friendship beyond repair. But they hadn't. They'd given in to temptation, and now he'd have to find a way to make sure that she knew she was still his everything, and that things would be okay. He didn't want her to feel used.

He was a bastard. A sick bastard.

And then things had gone from awkward to awkward as hell when he picked her up at her house that morning. She'd been waiting for him on her porch, and they hadn't texted each other like they normally did. He'd gone all morning with just a cup of coffee while he got Daisy ready for school and hadn't heard a word from his best friend. If he didn't find a way to fix this soon, he honestly didn't know how he would keep going. Adrienne was tangled in every facet of his life, and he'd always treasured that. If he lost it…hell, he wasn't sure how he'd figure out what to do.

They'd made pleasant conversation about the weather—purposely not talking about storms or hard rain—and about what projects they had that day. They'd also talked about the fact that Carter had already been by the parking lot to take Adrienne's car into his shop that morning before Mace had even woken up since the man worked strange hours. The two of them hadn't said a word about what had happened between them, and he knew if he wanted to fix this, he needed to say something. But what to say without putting his foot into his mouth or getting kicked in the balls like he rightly deserved? He had no clue, but he *had* to say something to fix this.

Now, after a few hours of working with Shep up front doing a full back piece, and Ryan on the phone dealing with someone who needed a first-timer appointment, Addi sat in her chair, working on a sketch for her next client. Mace figured that once the other two left for the day, he could figure out what he needed to say before he and Adrienne closed. He was an adult, damn it, he could do this. It wasn't as if he hadn't had sex before. But it had been the first time with his best friend—hence why he was acting like a lunatic.

Ignoring the pressing need to do *something* about

what had happened, he went to his bench and started working on his next project. It was a full back piece for a retired Master Sergeant who had gone without ink for his entire time in the service. Mace knew this was beyond important for the man and wanted to make it perfect, so he was taking his time and putting his best efforts into the work.

A hand rubbed something on his arm, and he started, looking over his shoulder before freezing.

Adrienne stood behind him, her eyes wide, and her hands in the air. "You had jam on your shirt."

He blinked and then shifted on his stool so he faced her, even though he had to look up to see her face. "Oh, uh, it was a tough morning getting everything ready for Daisy and her lunch and all that."

Laughter danced in her eyes before it burned away, replaced by that now-familiar awkwardness. "Well, it's gone now."

He cleared his throat, trying to get the memory of her touch out of his mind. She'd barely grazed his shoulder to wipe jam off it, yet his body had heated from just the thought of her so near. They had to fix this, and soon.

"Uh, can you grab a cup of coffee with me?" The unsaid *"we need to talk"* lingered between them.

She tilted her head, studying his face before nodding slowly. "Okay. Let me get my bag."

She left him, and he went to get coffee orders from the others, pointedly trying not to look Shep in the eyes as he did. Might as well make this excuse to talk to Adrienne a real thing.

"We each have clients in thirty minutes, so we should get a move on. Colorado Icing, or the deli?" Colorado Icing was Thea's bakery and had way better coffee. When he said as much, Addi smiled, but it didn't reach her eyes. He *had* to fix this.

They didn't have to go far before they went back inside, so he gripped her arm, stopping them both before they did. "We need to talk."

She stuck her hands into the pockets of her jacket and rocked on her feet. "I figured."

He had no idea what he should say to make it better, so he rambled, hoping to hell that somewhere in his random words were the right things.

"It was a one-time thing, right? Because we're best friends, Addi. If we fuck this up, I don't know what I'll do. It was a mistake to do what we did without talking about it first. It was stupid. I don't want to risk you, Addi. We're not only starting off a new company together, but you're also my boss, and now I'm a full-time dad, and hell, I'm not saying anything right, but we can't risk what we have. What we have is special, and I don't want to risk it. Because if we fuck everything up, it's going to suck beyond anything. You're my best friend, Adrienne. The one person, outside of my family, in my life that's a constant. I don't want what happened with us to end up being such a mistake that we lose what we have."

Her eyes narrowed, and her jaw clenched before she finally spoke. "First, you call what we did a *mistake* again, and I'm going to have to dick-punch you. We cannot do this again, and we will never talk about it, but never, *ever* call me—or any woman for that matter—a mistake to her face. Are we clear, Knight?"

He ran a hand over his face. "Jesus Christ, I'm not saying anything right." He took a deep breath before cupping her face and looking into her eyes. "I fucking loved every single moment I was with you, Addi. Every single damn second. But we should have talked beforehand and, apparently, right now, I'm not making much sense to talk afterward. I don't know what's coming next, nor do I know if we should even take this to...well, anything, but what I do know is that I want you in my life no matter what. I'll do anything to keep from losing you. Anything."

She leaned into his hold, her body relaxing as she let out a breath of her own. "I know it was just the heat of the moment and the crazy weather or whatever, but I loved it, too. And I don't know what we should do about it other than maybe not try to do it again while acknowledging it was pretty damn amazing sex?"

An older woman glared at them as she went to her car, but he didn't care. They were outside in the middle of a shopping area having this discussion, but it couldn't wait.

"So, we don't forget or ignore that it happened, but we also try to not let it happen again without actually talking to each other about it?"

She nodded. "Does that mean it *could* happen again?"

He licked his lips, aware that if he said the wrong thing this time he could lose her. "Maybe? I don't know, Addi. Everything I said about you being my boss and me trying to figure out how to be a full-time dad was true."

"And I'm super busy with trying to keep my head above water as we get through the first six months of the shop. But…"

He nodded. "But it was damn good."

"Of course, it was damn good. It's the two of us."

He lowered his head, resting his forehead on hers. "I'm not going to say the m-word again, but let's not fuck things up."

"We have no idea what we're doing," she whispered. "No clue."

"Nope. But let's keep doing it."

He didn't know what on earth that even meant, but they were in this together, and he just prayed that he didn't screw things up even more.

CHAPTER FIVE

Adrienne arched her hips, her hand between her legs as she imagined Mace's rough beard scraping her thighs as he ate her out. Despite how hot her imagination had gotten before, knowing exactly what his tongue on her pussy felt like now just made touching herself even hotter. She slid her fingers between her folds, pumped one, then two fingers in and out of herself before pulling out so she could slide her wetness over her clit. One hand cupping her breast, she pleasured herself until she came, her body shaking as the orgasm slammed into her, making her tingle all the way from her toes to her ears and the tips of her breasts.

"I'm going to Hell," she whispered, her hand still lazily stroking her clit. "So going to Hell."

It had been two days since she'd had the best sex of her life with her best friend, and though they'd had a conversation about it, she was still just as confused as ever.

What they had talked about:

1. The sex was amazing.
2. They probably shouldn't do it again.
3. The sex was amazing.
4. They were probably going to do it again.
5. The sex was amazing.
6. They could ruin everything because the sex was amazing.

She laid back, her hand falling to the side as she fought to catch her breath. Her morning routine of getting herself off was now far more complicated than it should be thanks to Mr. Big Dick and Fuck-tastic Hips.

And if she ever actually called him that to his face, she'd die of mortification.

She shouldn't be thinking about Mace and sex at all. She *should* be getting over her lapse in judgment and start focusing on work and family as usual. Instead, she was lying in bed before her alarm went off, making herself come by thinking about Mace's talented tongue replacing her fingers.

Again, going to Hell.

Sighing, she rolled out of bed, grabbed her phone so she could turn off her alarm, and promptly almost fell because her panties were still wrapped around her ankles.

Grace, thy name is Adrienne Montgomery.

She kicked off her panties and slogged her way to her bathroom so she could get ready for the day. Of course, she couldn't look at her counter without blushing and pressing her legs together. She'd *just* come, yet just looking at where Mace had fucked her had her ready to go again.

"I guess that's why I have that showerhead," she mumbled and went to sin once more thinking of Mace between her legs, this time using the hot water instead of her hands. "*So* going to Hell."

Her body ached, and she was pretty sure her nether regions would forever be swollen and needy thanks to thoughts of Mace, but she was finally in the parking lot to open the shop and in desperate need of caffeine. Maybe today would be different, and she wouldn't want to simultaneously fuck her best friend and hide from the situation at the same time.

Nothing good ever came from having sex with friends.

Nothing.

Except for those fantastic orgasms, but she was *not* thinking about those. Again. She had work to do, damn it.

Adrienne did her best to forget what she'd done that morning—or *any* morning—while thinking about Mace and climbed out of her car. Her brother-in-law, Carter, had replaced something inside, and for the life of her, she couldn't remember what. She could fix so many damn things in her house and at the shop if needed but tell her a car part, and she forgot the information instantly. Regardless, Carter had told her that the car was on its last leg, but he'd do his best so she could keep driving it. She liked that brother-in-law of hers, even when he gave her terrible news about what she already knew was a lost cause.

She was just about in front her shop when she froze, aware that there were a few other business owners staring at the tattoo shop, as well.

"Oh my God," she whispered, her phone clutched in her hand as she tried to reconcile what exactly she was seeing.

"Adrienne!" Thea called, running toward her, her own phone in hand. "I was just about to call you. I'll call Shep now. I'm so sorry, honey. I don't know what those lunatics were thinking."

Adrienne nodded, letting her younger sister mother her like she enjoyed doing. All she could do was stare at her store and what the monsters had done to it.

Bright red and green paint along with black and blue covered the front of the shop in splotches. Someone had used a red can of spraypaint to mark the windows up with slurs and other curse words that would forever be imprinted in her brain. Sure, she used the words *bitch* and *fuck* in her own vocabulary, but seeing it emblazoned starkly on her shop in contrast to the beautiful backdrop of the foothills and the pristine paint of the other buildings made it all the more terrifying.

Someone had tagged her shop and had done a hell of a job with it.

She couldn't quite think of what to do as Thea called the police and explained what had happened. Adrienne should be the one doing that, not her sister. It was her shop, after all. Hers and Shep's.

And someone had defaced it.

Strong hands slid around her waist, and she turned,

fist ready to punch, but stopped when she realized it was Mace.

"What the fuck, Addi?" he asked, but since he was looking at the shop and not her, she knew his words weren't about her almost hitting him but what had happened to their place of business.

"I don't know." She swallowed hard then got over herself because she had shit to do and a business to save. "But we're going to find out." She turned to Thea. "Cops on their way?"

Her sister nodded. "Yes, they said don't go in or touch anything. Just in case."

Adrienne nodded, not bothering to pull away from Mace's hold as he gave her strength that she desperately needed at that point. She wouldn't turn away someone to lean on when she needed it most. At least, that's what she hoped was the reason.

"Okay, I'll call Shep. Mace, can you call Ryan? Get him here if you can. Once the cops are done taking statements or photos or whatever, we need to start cleaning up. We have clients to work on today, and there's no damn way we are leaving it like this if we can help it."

"Adrienne..." Thea started, but she shook her head.

"Thank you for everything," she said and then looked at the crowd of well-meaning people, including their newest resident, the tea shop owner from next door. "Go back to work, everyone. I'm sorry this might hurt your business for the day but, hopefully, we'll get to the bottom of it."

She was so pissed. There was already a stigma surrounding her type of shop in this area, and now it was the one place tagged by whoever thought they would have some fun for the night. She wished she could start cleaning it off immediately and forget about it so she could get on with her day, but there were procedures to follow, and that meant she had to wait.

But waiting wasn't something she wanted to do.

Abby, the owner of Teas'd, the organic tea shop that had opened up right before Montgomery Ink Too, walked over with two mugs of what Adrienne guessed was tea.

"White chocolate peppermint," Abby explained. "A favorite right now. Drink and wait for the police to come. I know this sucks, but whenever you're allowed to start cleaning, we're all here for you." She looked around, and the other business owners, including Thea, nodded. "We're a team around here. And we don't take kindly to someone hurting one of us."

Adrienne gratefully took the tea and took a careful sip, her eyes nearly bugging out of her head. "This is amazing."

Abby winked. "I'm slowly turning everyone from the dark side of coffee."

"You're well on your way with this," Mace said from her side. He'd let go of her hip when Thea was talking, and Adrienne had been grateful since her sister was far too perceptive for her own good.

Despite Adrienne telling everyone to leave, they all stayed until the cops came to take photos and statements. Shep and Ryan had shown up soon after, the anger on their faces almost palpable. When the police left, saying they'd be in touch and that everyone could start cleaning up, Adrienne didn't feel any steadier. In fact, she still felt just as angry, hurt, and lost as before, but now, she had a list in place of what she had to do. Someone had dared to hurt the Montgomerys, and she'd be damned if she let that take her down. They'd find who did it, and then...well, she'd let the cops handle it from there. But she'd make sure her shop shone like a beacon of hope and art because there was no way she was going to let some asshole with paint ruin all her hard work. Not this time.

Soon, she found herself on the phone with a client who had been scheduled that morning but who she knew she'd have to move until later. It would take the whole crew to clean up the mess the vandals had made, and she honestly didn't want to have her clients seeing the place as it looked now. Thankfully, they hadn't broken any windows or done anything that looked too permanent. Power washing in a Colorado October wouldn't be fun, but at least it wasn't snowing. They'd scrub, power wash if needed, and paint. Luckily, they already had the paint in the back storage area because they'd just finished the place and had leftovers.

Her shop hadn't even been open a full month before someone tried to ruin it. She did her best not to take that to heart.

An arm wrapped around her shoulders as soon as she hung up with her client, and she leaned into her big brother's hold. She'd know his hugs anywhere. Shep was a few years older than Adrienne, and the only boy in their immediate family. He'd moved to New Orleans so long ago that it was odd seeing him back in Colorado Springs. He used to hang out with Austin in Denver on the weekends when they were growing up because he'd been so much older and hadn't wanted to only play with his sisters. Adrienne hadn't minded because that meant she could spy on what the boys were doing with Thea and Roxie whenever Austin visited them. It was what little sisters did, after all.

Now, though, her brother was all grown up and back home with his wife and child. Adrienne was so damn happy that she could be an aunt in person rather than through video chat, but even the idea of holding Livvy couldn't really make her smile feel real just then.

"How you holding up?" Shep asked before kissing the top of her head. His beard was long enough now to tangle in her hair and she pulled away, squinting her eyes at him.

"I'm fine. We're going to be fine. We just need to do the things on this list, and then we can open for the day."

Shep shook his head. "I don't think we're opening today, hon. Tomorrow for sure, but today? I think by the time we get all of this shit off the walls and clean ourselves up, the day will be almost over, and we'll be too physically and emotionally drained to do much else."

"We'll do a grand re-opening," Ryan said, holding a stack of buckets with a hose wrapped over his shoulder.

"You can't do that three weeks after the first one," she said quietly, then moved to help him and take some of his load. "Where's Mace?" She hadn't seen him since he held her to his side when he'd first shown up. She'd had plans to talk to him today about what... well, she really hadn't known how that talk would go, but now she was pretty sure it wouldn't happen this afternoon. Maybe ever. Not with everything going on. Mace had been right, their lives were far too complicated already to add more things that could ruin everything.

Ryan lifted his head and pointed with his chin. "Getting the rest of the stuff out of his truck."

"On it," Shep said and jogged out of the store toward where Mace had parked. Others had started to come out and help as well, and as much as Adrienne was grateful for that, she also really didn't want anyone else to see what had happened to her place. She *hated* that it was so public, and while some people were nice about it, others were giving her looks that were far too pitying for her state of mind.

And now she was just being whiny, and she hated that. So she rolled her shoulders back and headed out to help Mace unload his truck. He and Ryan had offered to gather everything while she and Shep worked at the store to deal with clients and starting the cleanup with what they had.

As soon as she held her bucket and sponge in her hand and Mace stood hip-to-hip with her, she let out a breath, staring at the words on her walls that seemed to grow larger and brighter against the cream color of the original paint job with each passing moment.

Mace leaned down and whispered in her ear, his warm breath sending shivers of sensation down her spine. "You've got this, Addi. You're not alone."

Unconsciously, she leaned into him, aware that her brother was staring at her but not truly caring at the moment. To the outside world, she and Mace were friends, and her leaning on him wasn't unusual. At least, that's what she hoped.

"We can do this," she said. "Because we have to."

"You know it, babe. You know it."

By the time they'd cleaned every inch of the face of her shop as well as part of Teas'd that had been defaced, as well—something she hadn't realized until they'd gotten a closer look—the five of them were dirty, grubby, and covered in filth and paint. Abby hadn't backed away when Adrienne had told the other woman they would handle her cleanup. Instead, she'd gotten dirty right next to them and had only just left to pick up her daughter from the sitter's. Adrienne didn't know the woman well, but she knew enough to know that her daughter's father was no longer in the picture, though she didn't know the whys and hows of it. Only rumors and she wasn't sure she could trust those.

Shep had been forced to leave as well because it was his afternoon with Livvy since Shea had to work, and Adrienne had told Ryan to go home, too. Her brother had been right. There was no way they would be able to open for the few short hours left in their long workday, so she'd given in and told herself she wouldn't cry until she was home alone with some wine and her bathtub.

Soon, she found herself alone in her shop with just Mace, and though she knew they needed to talk, she couldn't help but wrap her arms around his middle and bury herself in his hold. She needed her best friend more than anything after a day like this, and he knew it.

"It's going to be okay, Addi. Everything looks brand new, and we'll be back in business tomorrow." He ran his hand down her back and kissed the top of her head. And though Shep had done the same earlier, there was nothing brotherly about the way Mace held and touched her.

"It just sucks. I want to wallow for a bit." She clung to him harder and sighed. "Do you need to pick up Daisy soon?"

"She's at school for a couple more hours, then my parents are picking her up. They like being more involved now that they get to see her more often, and Daisy likes the time with them. The routine is settling her because, sometimes, I have no fucking clue what I'm doing."

She frowned and looked up at him. "You're doing pretty good, Mace. You're going from a weekend a month to full-time, and putting your all into it. *And you're letting your family help. I know those sisters of yours would be down here in a minute if you asked them to come.*"

Mace had two sisters who lived up in Denver. They had already come down the weekend before to hang out with Daisy, but they worked long hours and couldn't make the hour-long drive every night, though she knew they wanted to.

"You're pretty smart. Did you know that?"

She batted her eyes. "Of course, I know that."

He grinned then surprised the hell out of her by lowering his mouth to hers and kissing her. His tongue swept along the seam of her lips, and she opened for him, craving him more than she ever thought possible.

"The door locked?" he asked, his voice rough. His hands cupped her face, and she had to blink slowly so she could catch up with his words.

"Yes?"

"Was that an answer, or a question?" he teased before biting down on her lower lip.

She sucked in a breath and pulled away, though she still kept her hands on him. "The front door is locked, and we have the shades down, but what exactly is it that you're asking?"

"I'm not really asking anything. But I'm *thinking*

about taking you into that storage closet back there and having my way with you so you get your mind off all the shit going on right now." He kissed her again. "That's what friends are for, Addi. And that's what I am, no matter what else happens with us, I'm your *friend*."

She swallowed hard, not knowing what to say to that, so she kissed his jaw so he'd lower his head and allow her to take his lips. When he gripped her ass and lifted her up so she could wrap her legs around his waist, she knew they might be making a mistake once again, but she couldn't help her need for him.

She didn't know what would come next when it came to Mace Knight, but she honestly couldn't stop herself from needing him.

Not any longer.

No matter the cost.

CHAPTER SIX

Mace set Adrienne down on a stack of boxes in the storage room so he could close the door behind them. They were the only two left in the shop, and though the front door might be locked, Shep had a key. Having the man walk in on what Mace was about to do to his sister wouldn't be the best thing for Mace's health.

"Shirt off," he ordered, tugging it over her head.

"We're covered in paint and dirt and who knows what else. This is probably like the *worst* time to be getting each other off."

He lowered his head, kissing that sweet mouth of hers. "So I'll suck your nipples and your cunt, then I'll fuck you hard. No need to lick anything that has paint on it."

She raised her brow but reached around to undo her bra. The lace fell down onto her lap, leaving her breasts bare to his gaze. He loved the sight of her nipples, all rosy and pink against the paleness of her skin. She had script and branches on her side and cupping one breast, and he couldn't help but trace the design.

He'd been the artist, after all, and it had been the hardest project of his life. Not only because it was for his best friend but also because he'd had the most unprofessional hard-on the entire time.

"I love this tattoo."

She slid her hand up his side underneath his shirt. "My artist is pretty damn amazing."

His hand traced the rest of her ink before cupping her breast. "Yeah, he is."

She laughed and then moaned as he tweaked her nipple. "You're supposed to say something along the lines of how amazing your canvas was."

He bent over, licking one nipple then the other. "You know I love your skin." He kissed in between her breasts, kneeling between her legs. "Your taste." Lick. "The feel of you." Stroke. "The heat of you." Bite.

Before he could lick any farther down, however, she pushed him back and stood up. "As much as I *really* want your mouth on my pussy, there's something I need to do first."

He raised a brow, then grinned when she went to her knees instead and tapped his hip. "Oh yeah?"

"On your feet, Knight. I'm going to need that cock in my mouth. Like now."

She licked her lips as she looked up at him, and he had to take a deep breath so he wouldn't come in his jeans. How she did that to him every damn time she was near his dick, he didn't know, but he was starting to get a complex.

Together, they undid his pants, their fingers fumbling. He'd never known he would be able to handle laughing when a woman was so close to his cock but, apparently, Adrienne brought out the best in him. Soon, his pants were down over his hips, and a wet heat surrounded his length. He slid his hand through her hair, his balls tight as she sucked him off.

"Jesus, Addi, that mouth of yours."

She winked and opened her mouth slightly wider, then relaxed her tongue and swallowed more of him. His grip tightened in her hair, and he couldn't help but rock in and out of her mouth. She kept herself open for him, and he quickened his pace, fucking her mouth gently enough that he wouldn't hurt her but with enough vigor that the tip of his cock touched the back of her throat. The fact that she *let* him do that and moaned while he did, made it damn hard not to blow his load right there. But he didn't want to come in her mouth, not then. He needed to be inside her and make sure she came, too. So though it wasn't easy, he pulled out, leaned down, and picked her up under her shoulders and brought his mouth to hers. The taste of those little drops of come from the tip of his dick on her tongue stole a growl from him, and he rocked into her, his wet cock leaving a trail on her bare stomach.

"I wasn't done," she panted, her body clinging to his. Her breasts were bare, pressing into his chest, and all he wanted to do was suck on her nipples until they were bright and shiny and aching for him.

So he bent low and took one into his mouth, sucking and nibbling until she squirmed in his hold. Only when she was shaking in his arms did he let go and lick his way over to her other one, repeating the process.

"Mace…I need…I need."

He lifted his head, claimed her lips, and growled in her ear, "I know what you need."

He quickly pulled the condom out of his back pocket that he'd put there since he knew he wouldn't be able to hold back from Adrienne for too long, then turned her around so her breasts were against the wall in front of them. He quickly sheathed himself with the condom and shucked his pants down to his knees so he'd have more freedom to move.

"What are you doing?" she asked, her voice breathy. "I thought you wanted to play with my tits."

He moved her hair out of the way and sucked on her mouth. "Your nipples are already wet and cherry red from my mouth." He pressed her top harder into the wall as he slid his other hand in front of her so he could undo her jeans. "How do they feel against the coolness of the wall? Can you feel every inch of yourself, wet and aching?"

Her head fell back, and he licked the other side of her neck. "You're diabolical. Now get that cock inside me."

When her pants and panties were down below her luscious ass, he slid his cock between her cheeks and thrust. "One day, I'm going to take this ass of yours. Is it cherry? Because I damn well hope so, baby. I want to be the first inside you, the first taking you in every way possible."

"Just get in me already." She paused. "Not my ass. Not...not yet. But inside my pussy? Yes, let's do that."

She moved her head to the side so he could capture her lips, then pulled back, spreading her from behind so he could slam into her wet heat with one thrust. She clamped down around him, and they both froze, his body breaking out in a sweat just from the feel and temptation of her.

"Oh, damn," she moaned, her head falling back onto his shoulder. "I forgot how big you are."

"Am I stretching you?" he growled. "Stretching that tight pussy? Are you going to have to walk carefully tomorrow so no one knows you let my big, fat cock into that cunt of yours?" He thrust in and out of her, tiny strokes that sent heat up his spine and down to his balls.

"I never knew you were such a dirty talker, Mace."

He kissed her again, increasing his speed as he fucked her hard into the wall. "Turns out there's more to know about me, Addi. Want to give it a try?"

She blinked at him, her cheek pressed into the wall along with the rest of her as he pounded into her sweet body. "I, uh...yes? Yes, I want to try."

Mace swallowed hard then dug his fingers into her hips as he sped up, her ass pressed out, meeting him thrust for thrust until they were both calling out each other's names, their limbs shaking as they came. Her pussy spasmed around him almost painfully, and he knew she'd be sore tomorrow from the way he'd taken her. And though he never wanted to hurt her, the idea that she'd be marked in some way by his touch made him want to fuck her all over again. He was a caveman through and through right then, but then he remembered the fact that he still bore her marks on his back, a sign that he wasn't the only one who wanted to claim.

They stood there, his cock still deep inside her, leaning against the wall as they both fought to catch their breaths.

"Did we just…did we just say we're trying this?" she whispered. "Or was that just me saying it?"

He slowly pulled out of her so he could turn her around. This was a conversation they needed to face each other for. "It wasn't just you, but…" He swallowed hard. "I told you before, we can't ruin what we have."

She reached out and cupped his jaw. They were both mostly naked, though for some reason he still had his shirt on, and he still had the used condom on his cock. They couldn't have looked more awkward, yet he didn't care, not when what they were saying meant so much more than what position they were currently in.

"Then we don't ruin it. We keep doing what we're doing."

"Best friends who have great sex?" he asked cautiously. "Because we can't say there're no feelings. There will always be feelings when it's the two of us."

"Feelings, yes. But we can make sure we don't go into anything with more promises than we're willing to keep."

He lowered his head, pressing his mouth to hers. "Just you and me then. Whatever this is, however long we add this part to who we are, just you and me." The idea of her with another man right then made him want to scream, and that was something he was going to have to think about when he was alone. Because there was no such thing as casual sex, not when it came to the two of them.

"Deal." She looked down between them and grinned. "And I guess we should clean up because we don't really look like we're doing inventory, do we."

"I could make a joke about taking your inventory, but that seems a little crass, even for me."

She rolled her eyes and pushed at his chest so he backed up, careful not to trip over his pants since they were still around his ankles.

"Just don't leave the condom in the trashcan in here. Kind of hard to keep what we have just between us if we're leaving sperm everywhere."

He shook his head and took care of the condom as he dressed, his eyes on her movements as she put herself back to rights. Once again, he knew they were most likely making a mistake, but he didn't say anything. His craving for Adrienne was becoming an obsession, and that was something he had to work through—mistake or no.

The next morning should have been more awkward than it was, but for some reason, they were acting as if nothing had happened all the while Mace *knew* something was different. If he hadn't been confused before, he sure as hell was now.

Shep was already working on a tattoo that would probably take the whole day and was in the zone. He had music in one ear while his client slept since it was a back tattoo and, apparently, some people could sleep through anything as soon as the endorphins hit.

Ryan was coming in later for the closing shift and was really working well as part of their core group. It didn't always work out that way. Their old shop hadn't had the cohesive unit this one had, but Ryan was not only talented, he was also quickly becoming their friend.

Adrienne was working on a walk-in shoulder tattoo that would take an hour, max. She was bent over the bench, her concentration on her work as she bit her lower lip and focused. He did his best not to make it look like he was ready to bend her over just a bit more and take her from behind at the sight of her biting that delicate flesh.

While everyone else was working, Mace waited for his client to show up. He was already twenty minutes late, but Mace wasn't surprised. He was one of his regulars from the old shop and was constantly late. Hence why Mace always padded the time around whenever the appointment was set for. George, the client, made up for the time cost-wise, so Mace didn't mind too much, but it still left him pacing a bit because he wasn't exactly sure when the guy would actually show up. It annoyed the hell out of Adrienne, but Mace just dealt with it. It wasn't like he could control what George did, and honestly, he didn't want any other artist messing with his ink.

"George running late again?" Adrienne asked as she leaned back from her work and cleaned it off.

Mace nodded and then went into Adrienne's workspace to see the finished product. "Dude. That's fantastic."

She held up her hand, shaking her head. "Don't say another word until Tracy here gets to see it." She smiled as she said it, and Mace rolled his eyes. She had a thing about not saying anything about a tattoo until the client saw it, and while Mace agreed, he also wanted the world to know how talented his wo—best friend was.

Hell, he'd almost called her *his woman*.

She wasn't his, not like that. And because they'd set their flimsy boundaries, she never would be. They were best friends who now had sex—though only with each other. And, apparently, they were keeping it secret, which he agreed with because he didn't want to have to deal with all the knowing glances and endless questions that were bound to pop up when it came to the two of them. Everyone always wondered if they'd gone to bed together, and now that they had, he felt like everyone could tell.

And....now he'd ended up back in high school. He needed to get over himself.

Tracy, a middle-aged woman with bright eyes and long, auburn hair, bounced off the bench and practically skipped to the long mirror at the end of the pathway between the booths. Mace met Adrienne's gaze, holding back a smile. Tracy was far too energetic after having a needle stabbed into her arm over and over...but to each his or her own.

Adrienne handed Tracy a mirror so she could look at her ink, and the woman squealed as if she were a fifteen-year-old girl rather than a woman in her forties. The work on her shoulder was exquisite. Addi had added shadow and depth to the vibrant blues and purple hues to make it look as if the fairy were floating right off Tracy's shoulder and whispering a joke to anyone who passed by. For a walk-in without a lot of direction, Addi had knocked the art out of the park. Each of them at the shop had specialties, and she was coming into her own with this type of artwork for sure.

"I love it. It's the perfect fairy. Is it a good fairy? A bad one? Depends on the day. My husband is going to pass out when he sees it. I can't wait to surprise him." She shook her hips and did a little dance, and Mace couldn't help but laugh along with her. The woman's enthusiasm was infectious.

By the time Tracy had left, her laugh still echoing off the walls, Shep was still focused on the full back piece, just getting back from a water break, Adrienne was cleaning up her station, and Mace was finally getting down to work with George. They were working on a full-color piece on the man's thigh today, and Mace wanted to get started so he could get in the zone.

George was all set up in the chair, and Mace rolled his shoulders, ready to get started on the back-aching part. He'd be working on the outline today and would do the colors and final shading during their next appointment. It would be too much on both of their bodies to do the full art in one go. George's skin tended to swell, too, so Mace didn't want to screw up the end game by going too fast and too hard.

Adrienne came up to him while he was about thirty minutes in and took the extra stool in the booth. Though the heat of her next to him made him harden slightly, he was professional enough to keep his eyes and attention on his work and not the woman next to him.

"Looking good, George."

The other man gave her a wink from his perch on the chair. "You know it. I only want the best."

Adrienne raised a brow, and Mace did his best to hold back his smile. George was a great guy but, sometimes, he didn't think before he spoke. Between that and his inability to be on time, Mace sometimes wondered why he liked working on the man as much as he did.

George seemed to understand that he'd stepped in it and quickly backtracked. Mace had to sit up, lifting the needle since the other man's thigh had tensed as he put his hands up in the air in surrender.

"I meant...shit. I didn't mean you weren't the best. Just that Mace is one of the best. You're the other best."

Shep cleared his throat behind them, and Mace couldn't help but join in with Adrienne's laughter. "I'm standing right here, you know," his boss and friend said with mock sternness. "I mean, come on."

"You're fine, George." She patted his arm, her smile wide. "Just know that while Mace is the best. I'm the bestest of the best."

Mace kicked her foot. "Whatever you say, babe. The answer's in the ink."

She snorted and leaned into his shoulder, and he swallowed hard, doing his best to back away slowly and not let Shep see his true reaction. Mace and Adrienne had always touched and leaned into one another, but things were different now. He'd known that things would change once they slept together, and though they'd each said that nothing would happen outside of what they did in the bedroom, it had been a lie. A necessary lie, but a lie nonetheless. And with Shep so close to them and observant beyond measure, the two of them were walking a dangerous line that he wasn't sure either of them knew how to fully straddle without ramifications.

Before he could get too lost in his head, the door opened again, and everyone looked toward the front area as a man in a suit holding a clipboard walked in, a frown on his face as he looked around.

"Is,"—the man looked down at the thick clipboard

in his hand—"there an Adrienne or Shephard Montgomery here?"

Mace straightened as Adrienne stood, wiping her gloved hands on her pants. "That would be me," she said, her voice friendly but firm.

"And me," Shep said, his voice a tad deeper than usual.

Ever since that unknown man had come into MIT and threatened them, and then with the addition of the graffiti attack on their building, everyone had been on edge. Whoever this guy was, didn't give Mace a good feeling. And from the way Adrienne and Shep stood tense and yet professional, he wasn't the only one who felt that way. Even George and Shep's client seemed on alert since both of them were regulars and friends of the crew.

"Andrew Berry here," the man said, pulling out his wallet. "Department of Sanitation. We've had a couple of calls and complaints. I'll need to do an inspection, according to our code…"

The man rambled on about code numbers and what needed to be done, and Mace held back a curse. All three incidents so far might not seem connected since they were all out of the blue and different, but Mace didn't trust what was going on. MIT hadn't been open for long, and now they were dealing with this crap?

He quickly cleaned up George, knowing they wouldn't be able to finish today. The other man and Shep's client were understanding, but he knew if something didn't change, the shop would be dealing with even more issues soon. If word got out that they were having cleanliness issues as a tattoo shop? They'd be screwed.

"Go home," Adrienne said an hour later when Mr. Berry was done. "No use in you staying when we're so quiet for the night. Ryan's on his way in, and we're still open so he'll be able to finish an appointment." There was such defeat in her voice that Mace knew she probably needed time to herself so she could get through whatever was going on in her head before she faced the next step—whatever that was.

"I can stay. There's plenty of things to do. Though, thankfully, the list the asshole gave you wasn't that long." He didn't have anything on his schedule now at the shop since he should have been working on George. With that off the table thanks to the unplanned and unnecessary visit, he would only be working on walk-ins with Ryan and Adrienne.

She looked down at the paper in her hand and scowled. "There're two things on here and they aren't even marks, just suggestions for better practice. The man looked annoyed that he even had to come here at all and said he'd look into who thought it would be a good idea to waste his time, but it still pisses me off."

Shep leaned against the wall near them and frowned. "Someone is out to get us. That's what it feels like. And, yeah, it makes me sound like I'm talking about the mob or some shit like that but it took us four extra months to even get this place built, and now that we're here, we've had issue after issue, and all things that are meant to keep people away. I don't like this. Not one bit."

Mace didn't either, and it made him even more reluctant to leave. But with Adrienne so closed-off, and since the only way he knew to make her feel better was to kiss that frown off her face, he figured he should leave her with her brother and Ryan so she could think through her feelings.

"We'll figure it out," Adrienne said, still scowling. "We're Montgomerys. We don't take shit from other people."

"Hell yeah," Shep said before squeezing her shoulder and going up to the front where his next client was coming in. Thankfully, they hadn't had to cancel everything.

"I'll head home and hang with Daisy," Mace said. "Pick her up from the parents early." He nudged Adrienne with his shoulder. "I made stew in the Crock-Pot before I left, so come over when you're done since you're not closing. I'll even let you have the ends of the French bread I bought."

She laughed softly, and he relaxed. If she could laugh, even a little, then she'd be okay. He just hoped they could figure out exactly what was going on—at the shop and between them.

"Stew sounds good," she said.

Mace had known things would get complicated once they started this new path of their lives, but as things kept coming at them, he had a feeling he'd only scratched the surface of how things would be changing.

He nodded and then said his goodbyes before heading to his parents' so he could pick up Daisy. He was afraid he'd never be able to fully comprehend or appreciate how his life had changed. He now had her in his life every day rather than just on the phone when he wanted to talk to her.

"I like stew," Daisy said, peering over the counter as she stood on the tiny black and purple pop-up stool he'd bought at the hardware store. "It's warm and yummy in my tummy."

Mace couldn't help the laugh and shook his head. "Really? I like the potatoes the best. What about you?"

Daisy tapped her lips with her tiny finger as she thought hard about her answer. He loved that she made sure every answer she had was the right one—or at least the right words for the answer she had.

"I like the spicy things that aren't spicy." She tilted her head and studied the Crock-Pot. "What are those again?"

"That's the garlic. I like that, too." He held back his full laugh at her answer since it was so unexpected and yet so Daisy. "Maybe next time I'll make a horseradish sauce to add to the top."

Her little nose scrunched up. "A horse and a radish? Why would you make sauce with a horse? I don't want horsey sauce."

Mace took his time explaining exactly what horseradish actually was before picking her up and throwing her over his shoulder, her giggles making him settle down after a weirdly long day. Adrienne would be over soon, and they'd have dinner and try to enjoy the rest of their night without worrying about the other crap in their lives—or at least trying not to. He'd heard from Jeaniene every day since she left, surprising him, though it shouldn't have. She wanted to be a part of Daisy's life, but not the part that they'd planned on. He wasn't sure if he could ever forgive his ex for that, not that he'd ever forgiven her for taking Daisy away in the first place.

As his daughter skipped around the room, singing a

song she'd made up the day before, he did his best not to worry like he'd told himself he wouldn't. Only, as soon as the doorbell rang and Adrienne walked through the door, he knew he'd lied to himself.

He'd worry about every damn thing he was doing wrong, but right then, he'd have dinner with his two best girls and just be.

As much as he could.

CHAPTER SEVEN

With the week Adrienne had been having, if it weren't for getting off thanks to Mace and the upcoming Brushes With Lushes night, she was pretty sure she'd have screamed into her pillow.

And, yes, she'd put getting off with her best friend on top of her list.

She was a Montgomery with a weakness—Mace Knight in all his big-dicked glory.

Adrienne rested her head on her steering wheel and let out a silent scream. She had no idea what she was doing, and all she could do was make immature jokes about the size of Mace's cock to herself while counting down the hours until she could either get it in her mouth again or ride him until they were both spent.

This wasn't supposed to happen. She wasn't supposed to crave him like this. It was only supposed to be for one night or not at all. And now, every time she was near him, she had to do her best not to touch him, or worse, keep from staying away from him. If she did either too much, she'd break, or others would notice that something was different between the two of them.

"I have no idea what I'm doing," she said to herself, her voice oddly loud in the quiet car. "No freaking clue." But if she sat here in the parking lot talking to herself for much longer, she'd have to add going insane to her already long list of confusing things she'd done in the past month.

So instead of wallowing over who was out to get her shop, the sketch she couldn't get quite right for a cancer survivor who wanted to commemorate the occasion with a delicate yet fierce tattoo, and lamenting over what she was doing with Mace, she planned to enjoy her night out with her sisters and friends.

Tonight was Girl's Night, after all, and they were kicking off their second monthly Brushes With Lushes gathering. It was a night that consisted of painting and drinking wine, all while having fun with your friends, and being watched and guided under the careful—and usually patient—eye and hand of their instructor, Kaylee.

Adrienne had a decent eye when it came to painting, she was an artist, after all. Except her medium was ink and her canvas, skin, but in the end, she got to draw and play with pretty colors while hanging with the women in her life that made it all worth it.

Her sister Roxie was pulling in as Adrienne got out of her car, and she waited while Roxie parked and made her way over.

"Hey there. Are we late?" her sister asked as she hugged her close. "I hate being late."

Adrienne looked down at her watch and shook her head. "Nope. Right on time, but I bet you Thea, Abby, and Shea are already there since they tend to be early to everything like you." She gave Roxie's messy hair and incorrectly buttoned blouse under her unzipped coat a look. "Why are *you* not early?"

Roxie's cheeks reddened, and she gave her a shy smile. "Uh, Carter got off work early and, well..."

Adrienne laughed, wrapped her arm around her little sister's shoulders, and started her way toward the renovated warehouse where Kaylee had set up her studios. "Good to know you're still in the newlywed phase where you're all over each other." The two of them couldn't be more opposite from what Adrienne had seen, but she knew they were in love—even if it looked as if they'd rushed into their marriage. But it wasn't as if she knew exactly what was going on in their relationship, and as she was secretly banging her best friend, she had no room to talk.

"He's my Carter." Roxie let out a dreamy sigh that was so unlike the annoyed one she'd given last time she'd spoken of her new husband. "What can I say?"

"You're happy, so that makes me happy. Plus, he's a sexy mechanic so..."

Roxie laughed. "And he's *my* sexy mechanic. I'm glad he could fix your car."

Adrienne groaned as she opened the door to the warehouse. "For now. I'm going to have to suck it up and get a new one soon. Well, maybe not a new one, but a new*er* one than I have now."

"You've had that one for almost a decade. I'm surprised it's been running as long as it has." They put their coats on the rack near the door and went to the back where the Brushes With Lushes event was being held that night.

"It would have gone to the junkyard in the sky last year without Carter. So make sure you give him a kiss just for me." She winked. "I was going to say something like a hand job or something, but then I realized he's now my brother-in-law and he doesn't know me well enough for that."

Roxie just laughed and hip-bumped her. "I don't

think Carter needs any extra help getting those things. In fact, I'm going to end up needing a wrist brace at some point if I'm not careful."

And that was why the two of them were laughing so hard they were crying as they entered the paint room and took their seats alongside Abby, Thea, and Shea. Their mom had come with them the first time but had bowed out this week since she had date night with their dad. The fact that her parents still had date nights made Adrienne's romantic heart swoon. She might have put her career and art before her love life for far too long, but she believed in love and everything warm and bubbly about it.

"Do I want to know?" Thea asked, her voice taking on that motherly tone that fooled no one. Thea was just as dirty as the rest of them, even if she liked to boss them around lovingly.

"Probably," Adrienne said with a wink as she unwrapped her scarf. It was getting colder and colder every night, and she knew she'd have to switch out her fall coat for her winter one soon. She hated that, these days, she couldn't wear her cute leather one for longer periods since winter tended to creep up on them faster each year.

"Whoever came up with this idea was brilliant," Shea said as she sipped her red wine. Each of them usually only had a glass since they all had to drive, but it was fun to enjoy the time together regardless.

"I know," Abby agreed. She owned the tea shop, Teas'd, next door to MIT, and had been friends with Thea since she moved into the building a few months before Adrienne had. "I heard they're all over the country now, though, and since I've finally heard of them, they probably won't be popular for too much longer. I'm always the last to learn anything."

Adrienne snorted. "You're not alone. I never know what's the *in* thing to do these days, but wine and painting? I'm in."

"Better than your knitting?" Thea asked, her eyes twinkling.

Adrienne did her best to flip her sister off without anyone else noticing, but the older woman behind their crew stuck up her nose. Whatever. She and her sisters were the inked and pierced crew—even if two of their group were accountants who hid their ink thanks to their jobs—all of them were used to looks. They were Montgomerys, after all, and tended to stand out in a crowd.

"Knitting?" Abby asked. "You knit?"

Adrienne winced. "I tried. My cousin, Meghan, tried to teach me along with my other cousin-in-law, Jillian.

Jillian did a little better, but I faked my way through most of it."

Abby frowned, tilting her head as she studied them.

"What is it?" Roxie asked.

"You're talking about Meghan and Jillian Montgomery? Married to Luc and Wes respectively."

Adrienne sat straighter on her stool. "Yeah, Meghan and Wes are our cousins."

"We have like forty of them or something," Roxie put in dryly.

"How do you know them?" Shea asked.

A sad look crossed over the other woman's eyes before she blinked it away. "Oh, I know Murphy Gallagher, whose brother is married to Maya. Your cousin."

"Small world," Roxie said as the rest of them started talking about all the Montgomerys and their various spouses and babies. Adrienne could never keep up, and honestly, her mind was on what Abby had said and not what they were talking about.

She'd heard of Abby, and not just because she was part of the community Adrienne had moved into. But her story wasn't one that Adrienne thought she wanted anyone else to know, at least not yet, so she kept it to herself. But her heart ached for the other woman, even as she tried to keep the expression on her face sweet so

Abby wouldn't know that Adrienne already knew some of the horrors she had faced. And Adrienne figured she didn't even know the half of it.

Kaylee walked into the studio at that moment, pulling Adrienne out of her thoughts, and their evening of Brushes With Lushes finally began. Adrienne loved Kaylee. She was a few years older than Adrienne and had an air about her that said she'd been through it all, twice, and came out the other side stronger. Plus, she was a fantastic artist with such a depth of talent that if one didn't realize that helping others enjoy art was important, they'd wonder why she was wasting her time with an evening like this.

"Welcome all," Kaylee began with a smile. "I see the Lushes part of the evening is in full swing." She winked, and everyone held up his or her decorated wine glass in cheers. Each glass held a hand-painted saying on it, as well as cute decorations along the stem. Adrienne figured that either Kaylee had had fun one weekend painting, or they were from another event where people left them for others to enjoy. Either was possible, knowing the artist. "Now, let's get the Brushes part started."

She took the lace scarf off the painting on the easel beside her and while others gasped, laughed, or starting giggling, Adrienne narrowed her eyes in study.

This was the part she loved, and she wanted to make sure her art was the best it could be. While this wasn't a competition and no one would be truly comparing his or hers to each other's outside of joking, Adrienne was still an artist herself and didn't want to screw it up. This wasn't paint by numbers, and there was always wiggle room for originality as they went along, but Adrienne liked to get as close to the original as possible. It kept her skills up.

The moonscape in front of her was simple and beautiful. There were a few dark trees in the foreground, and the whites, purples, and blues would be fun to play with as they layered on. This was *so* much better than her failed knitting attempt. Meghan and Jillian might have thought she'd gotten the hang of it, but she'd had to practice hours and hours with no true progress, and she'd never been able to cast on correctly. Painting was totally in her wheelhouse, and so much fun to do when she was with her family and friends.

As everyone began, Shea and Abby bent their heads together, laughing at a joke at the end of their row, while Adrienne sat between a determined Thea and Roxie. Roxie had her tongue between her teeth as she tried her hardest to get the shapes right, and Adrienne knew it vexed her younger sister that, of the four siblings, she was the one who had the most problems with any kind of drawing or painting. Adrienne and Shep were tattoo artists, of course, but Thea was a baker who could decorate cakes and cookies like no one's business. They each had their own strengths, but she knew Roxie hated that hers wasn't the same as her siblings'.

"Why is this so hard?" Roxie mumbled, stabbing at her canvas.

"That's what she said," Thea and Adrienne said at the same time before breaking down into giggles.

Roxie's lips twitched before she joined them. "Such mature ladies," she said with a snort before setting down her brush so she could have more of her wine. "And can we do like a trivia night next time or something? I'd rock at that."

"If we do that, we'd have to invite Shep," Adrienne put in. "He only barely lets us have this night on our own."

"True," Shea said from the other end of the row. "He not only likes wine, but he enjoys painting, as well. It's only because we've banned the men from our Girls' Night gatherings that he's not sulking behind us at this very moment."

Adrienne couldn't help but smile. After a decade of having her big brother living across the country—okay, New Orleans wasn't *that* far from Colorado, but it sure as hell felt like it—she liked getting to know the adult Shep and all his idiosyncrasies.

"I'd still beat him," Roxie said, her chin held high even as laughter danced in her eyes. "I need to beat him at *something*."

Adrienne patted Roxie's shoulder. "You don't suck at this, you know." She waved at her sister's painting. "You just want things to be perfect, and something like this doesn't always need to be perfect."

Roxie stuck out her tongue before taking another sip of her wine and setting the glass down. "That's what Carter says, yet sometimes it's like none of you understand me." She rolled her eyes, making it a joke, but Adrienne couldn't help but wonder if there was more to her words—and not just about herself.

Adrienne turned a bit to meet Thea's gaze, but neither of them said anything in response to Roxie's statement. Whatever was going on with their sister and Carter wasn't their business—yet. Of course, for all she knew, nothing was going on at all, and she was just looking too hard beneath all of Roxie's words. After all, Carter was nothing but loving and caring when he was near the rest of the family, and even that evening, Roxie had come to the event looking wonderfully disheveled.

She took a sip of her drink, knowing she was only running in circles around her sister's marriage because it was easier to do than wondering what the hell she was doing with her own relationship.

They painted some more while talking about nothing important until Shea asked how Thea's best friend, Molly, was doing.

Thea set down her brush and frowned. "I don't know. She doesn't talk to me about Dimitri or how she feels about the divorce. She just acts like nothing is wrong and that this whole thing is just a new phase of her life."

Adrienne winced. "That doesn't sound good."

"I know, right?" Thea gulped the last of her wine before setting her glass down on the cloth-covered bench a little harder than necessary. Thankfully, the glass didn't break. "She's just going about her business, and I can tell that Dimitri is truly hurting, but it's not like I can talk to him about it or even be on his side because—"

"Because she's your best friend, and that means you're automatically on her side." Adrienne had already finished her wine and was on her second glass of water since she liked to hydrate, so she drank for a moment before letting out a breath. "I'm sorry you're in the middle."

This was another reason she stayed out of relationships. Everything was so complicated. Every single woman at this table had a ton of baggage and history when it came to love and men yet, somehow, Shea and perhaps Roxie had made it through to the other side. Thea was perpetually single just like Adrienne, and Abby? Well, that wasn't her story to tell.

"But I'm not in the middle, not really," Thea said, her sad gaze resting on her painting. "I can't be. Dimitri was my friend too, and now...well, now he can't be anymore, not the same way, and that sucks." She blew out a breath then went back to painting, the subject closed. Adrienne was fine with that. It wasn't as if she knew what to say to make it better, after all.

She purposely didn't bring up Mace and knew she was being a coward. It wasn't as if she had any idea what she would or *could* say if someone brought it up. Her sisters saw far too much, and Adrienne had a feeling Shea and Abby were the same way when it came to ferreting out information. They'd all gone through their own levels of connections, and she knew they'd use that experience to see right through her. Or maybe she was being far too cautious and nervous about what they would say once she mentioned Mace's name. After all, he was her best friend, and she was allowed to bring him up, especially since they also worked together. It wasn't as if she had to tell the world she was sleeping with him.

Often.

And not really sleeping.

Her muscles tightened at the thought of him, and she cursed her inner hussy. He was just as much of a harlot since he was constantly making her come, but again, she wasn't going to think about that...no matter how much she wanted to.

"So, big sister," Thea began, her voice far too casual. "You seem far too relaxed these days for opening a new business. Who's the guy?"

"Yes, you do look too well lubed," Roxie put in, a grin on her face.

"Trust you to make the mechanic joke," Adrienne said dryly. And she couldn't lie to her sisters, not well enough, so she told them part of the truth—the only part she could. "And, well...I *have* been sleeping with a guy. But no one you know. It's not that important. Just relieving some tension."

The others didn't ask her any other questions, but their gazes held far too many for her liking. Shea gave her a look, and Adrienne stiffened. As soon as the words had left her mouth, she'd known they were a mistake and far too hurtful, but she hadn't known how to make sure the others knew it wasn't serious. If Mace ever found out...

She stopped that line of thinking and went back to

painting. The others followed suit, and she hoped none of them noticed that her hand was shaking, just a tiny bit.

"So, how's the shop going?" Shea asked a bit later as they all left and headed to their cars. "I know Shep's been stressing out over whoever is trying to hurt MIT, but how do *you* think it's going?"

Adrienne tightened her scarf as she leaned against Shea's car. The others had already left the parking lot, leaving the two of them to talk in private. She wasn't sure any of them had meant for it to happen, but it was fine with her.

"Financially, the shop is doing great, as you know. We're getting in new clients daily, and we already have waiting lists for the major work coming in. But as for who wants to take us down? Other than that mystery man at the beginning, I have no clue. No matter who we ask around the building, no one knows who it could have been. That seems weird to me. To all of us."

Shea nodded. "I know. And I'm not from here, so it's not like I have any idea who could have ties to the area that would want your shop out of the way. I just hope all of you are safe, you know? I don't want anyone to get hurt."

Adrienne reached out and squeezed Shea's arm. "We're being careful. So careful that the boys have gone all caveman and don't let *anyone* walk to their cars at night alone. Even Thea and Abby if they can find a way to stop it."

"It helps that you and Mace are sleeping together, too. He's able to watch you more often."

"Well, yeah, but I don't really think that has anything to do with it." Adrienne shut her mouth quickly, her face heating as Shea looked like a cat in cream.

The other woman bounced from foot to foot and pointed. "I *knew* it. I knew it!" She danced around, wiggling her hips, and Adrienne felt all the blood leech from her face.

"How...you tricked me!" She growled at the other woman, but Shea just continued to do her insane hip-wiggle dance.

"Yes, I did. And I'm proud of it. I'm learning to be a Montgomery day by day." She stopped her dance—thankfully—and reached out to grip both of Adrienne's arms. "First, I'm happy for you. Second, I was only guessing because I got a vibe from you both last time I was in. Third, Shep has no clue. Fourth, I won't tell him because there's a code. However, a caveat to that is if he asks me directly for some unknown reason, I will have to tell him because I don't lie to my husband."

Adrienne let out a shuddering breath. "Just...just make sure he has no reason to ask you."

Shea moved forward and hugged her hard. "I'll do my best. I'm happy for you." She whispered the last part, and for some reason, tears stung the back of Adrienne's eyes.

"It's...it's nothing. It has to be nothing. Okay?"

Shea nodded, before frowning. "I get it. But, Adrienne? Don't call Mace unimportant again. I think you're doing both of you a disservice if you do that."

Adrienne didn't say anything as she watched the other woman get in her car and drive away, leaving Adrienne to stand there like a lying idiot who couldn't even come up with a good fib that didn't hurt anyone.

She got into her own car and looked down at her phone as it buzzed.

Mace: *You get home okay?*

She refused to feel warmth at his caring.

Adrienne: *I'm still in the parking lot. Wanted to talk to Shea a bit.*

She turned on her car before calling him on her Bluetooth. Her car might be old, but it still had at least that much since the tech wasn't *that* new.

"Sorry for calling, I just wanted to start home and didn't want to text and drive."

His deep grumble of a voice came through her speakers, and she was very afraid that she'd made a mistake in listening to him like this. Talk about a distraction.

"I'm glad you're not texting and driving. You have fun with the girls?"

She nodded, then remembered he couldn't see her. Hell, he was making her act loopy, and it had nothing to do with the single glass of wine she'd finished over an hour ago.

"It was a blast. And I have a pretty painting to put in my house."

His laugh went straight between her thighs. Damn man. "You're going to have a hundred of those one day and will end up giving a few to me."

"You sound as if you don't want them," she teased. "Just for that, you're getting this one."

"I'm honored," he said dryly, but she knew he was joking.

"Um…so I have to tell you something, and I don't really want to." She pulled onto her road, thankful that it wasn't a long drive for her since she really didn't want to be driving at all when she told him this. "Hold on, let me turn off my car so I can use my phone rather than let the whole neighborhood hear my conversation." She'd had that happen once, forgetting that her speakers could be heard even through closed windows, and she'd never lived it down.

"Okay," he said, drawing out the word. "Do I need to come and get you? Are you safe?"

She swallowed hard, her eyes stinging again as she put her phone to her ear. "I'm fine. I promise. But, well, the girls noticed that I looked, um, relaxed shall we say?"

Mace didn't say anything, the silence palpable.

"So, in other words, they knew I was sleeping with someone."

"And what did you say?" he asked, and she couldn't read his voice. She usually needed to see his eyes in order to guess his emotions and had never been really good at it through the phone.

"That, yes, I was sleeping with someone. Then I lied completely because I'm an idiot and said it was someone they didn't know and that the person wasn't important." She spoke quickly so he didn't have a chance to get a word in. "I knew it was the worst thing to say as soon as I said it because you're nothing but important to me, but I was stupid, and I'm so sorry I called you that. I know we're walking on eggshells as we figure out exactly what *this* is, and I shouldn't have called you unimportant like you were nothing. I'm so damn sorry. Oh, and Shea knows about us, by the way. Totally guessed it and got on my case for calling you what I did, but she promises not to tell Shep." She stopped talking, her breath coming in gulps of air as she realized she'd blurted out everything without actually taking a breath.

"Babe."

"Yeah?"

"That was a lot."

"I know."

"First, I get why you said it. Hell, I probably would have said the same thing and rambled to you right after. I know you think I'm important just as I hope you know that I think you're damn important to me. As for Shea? I figured someone would figure out one day since the two of us are constantly eye-fucking each other. Don't get me wrong, I love imagining you bent over various pieces of furniture at the shop, but if we want to keep this between us, then we might need to hold back from doing that. As for not telling Shep?" He paused. "Well, when we're ready to tell people what we're doing—once we figure it out, that is—I'll deal with whatever he has to say when it comes to it."

She rested her head on her steering wheel, aware

that she needed to get inside at some point. "This is getting complicated."

He was silent for so long that she was afraid she'd lost him.

"Yeah, it is, but we were complicated already."

"True. I just...I can't lose you as my friend, Mace."

"You'll never lose me, Addi. Even if we find ourselves just friends again, you'll never lose me."

At that odd statement, she sat up again, wondering what the hell she was doing.

"Goodnight, Mace."

He sighed. "Night, Addi girl."

Then there was silence again as the line cut off and she stared at her phone, wondering if their beginning was close to their ending...and if her best friend in all the world had just lied to her.

CHAPTER EIGHT

Mace couldn't help but grin as Daisy ran into his parents' arms, her words running into one another as she told them about her day. Everybody said kids were resilient, but the way Daisy had bounced back from that first day at his house to now was remarkable. She still talked to her mom every day on the phone and Skyped three times a week, but she'd settled into Mace's life and routine far easier than he would have expected.

"Hey, big brother."

Mace turned as Sienna made her way up the walkway, their other sister Violet right behind her. Both of the girls lived and worked up in Denver and didn't make the drive down to the Springs as much as they used to. Their monthly family dinners, however, weren't something anyone could get out of. And now that he had Daisy with him, he didn't really mind.

"Hey there." He wrapped one arm around her shoulder, the other around Violet's, and squeezed. "Missed you brats."

Violet pinched his side, and he winced. Her fingers were damn strong, and she'd had years of practice when it came to pinching him so the parents wouldn't notice. That's what siblings did, after all. And since they were in his arms, he gave each a gentle headlock, eliciting screeches from both of his sisters and a stern look from his mother.

He quickly let his siblings go, but not before giving them another squeeze. They were all well into their adult years, yet there was nothing more satisfying than playing around with Sienna and Violet like they had when they were kids. He wasn't ever the jerk big brother who picked on his sisters, rather he played back just as hard as they did to him, and their relationship worked. He'd hated when they'd gone off to college in Denver, and though it was only a little over an hour away, it had felt like farther since he didn't get to see them daily like he used to.

He followed the girls into the house and watched as his parents doted on his kid. They hadn't been happy with his ex when they realized what she'd done, but the fact that they had unfettered access to their grandchild now had largely made up for their ire.

"You're growing up so fast," Jeff, his father, said to Daisy, his laugh deep. "One minute, you can fit in the palm of my hand; the next, you're as tall as I am."

Daisy bounced from foot to foot, her grin from ear to ear. "I'm not *that* big, Grandpa. I still have lots of growed to do."

"Growing," Mace corrected and crossed his eyes at both of his sisters when their lips quirked. He didn't get to act like a dad around them often. Until recently, he hadn't had the time with Daisy that he wanted, so his family would just have to deal with this not-so-new side of him now. After all, he was getting used to his role in Daisy's life.

"Growing," Daisy repeated, beaming at Mace before turning back to her grandpa. "I'm a big girl now, though. Big, big, big."

Mace was lucky that she wasn't looking at him then because he was pretty sure his face had gone pale at the thought of how many years had already passed in her life. She still had years to go before she was making those new milestones as a teenager and beyond, but the fact that he might now be the sole person dealing with it all was beyond overwhelming. He had no idea what Jeaniene's next step was when it came to her job, or what would happen when she got back to the country in a few months, but he knew that, no matter what, he wouldn't let Daisy go without a fight. He'd been unable to do what was right the first time because he'd been out of his depth, and Jeaniene had been the one with all the power. But after what she'd done this time, his lawyer had assured him things would be different. He'd have to roll with whatever came when everything fell around him, but he wouldn't let his and Daisy's relationship go back to how it had been before this.

His mom, Dani, came up then and hugged each of them close. "There's my babies." He leaned down so she could kiss his cheek, and she patted his face. "Your beard is getting so long. I'm always afraid it's going to scratch me when I kiss your cheek, but it's so soft." She patted him again before glaring at his sisters, who rolled their eyes at him.

"He has a beard care routine," Sienna said with a grin. "All the lumbersexuals do."

"What's a lumbersex?" Daisy asked, and Mace glared at his sister, who had the grace to wince.

Mace reached down and picked up Daisy, setting her on his hip. She was almost too big to do this now, but he'd take her wanting him to hold her as long as he could.

"It's lumbersexual, and that's a made-up word from

people who don't understand beards." He shot a look at his other sister when she went to say something, probably countering his point with real facts, but he wasn't in the mood.

Daisy put her tiny hands on his face and gave him a solemn look that went straight to his heart. "I love your beard, Daddy. So if you don't want to be a lumbersex, don't be."

This time, neither Sienna nor Violet could keep their laughter at bay, and both of his parents joined in. He gave them all a mock scowl before blowing a raspberry on Daisy's neck. His little girl squealed before wiggling out of his arms.

"Don't use that word, okay, Daisy-cakes? It's a grown-up word."

"Okay. Like shit and damn, right? Mommy said those are bad words, but Aunt Adrienne said that once I'm the biggest girl, I can use them if they help my meaning. Or something like that."

"Daisy," he said sharply, and she looked down at her feet.

"Sorry."

He was going to have to strangle his best friend. And bite her. Yeah, biting would be good. And then he promptly shoved those thoughts from his mind since he didn't want to have a hard-on in front of his entire family.

"When you're a grown-up like me, you can use those words. How's that?"

She nodded, and Mace pointedly ignored the curious looks his sisters gave him at the mention of Adrienne. Neither of them had ever believed that he and Addi hadn't slept together before now, and since he was actually semi-seeing her currently, he knew he had to walk a fine line to keep that secret at bay.

"And now that that's taken care of," his mother cut in, "let's finish taking off our coats and go into the living room. I made those mushrooms you all like."

Daisy bounced on the balls of her feet, and Mace bent down to take off her little hat, scarf, and jacket. She'd been standing in the foyer with her outdoor stuff on for far too long as it was, and he didn't want her to get overheated. A cold front had rolled in overnight, and he had a feeling the winter was going to be a long one. His sisters took off their jackets, and he did the same, hanging his on the rack that had been on the same wall ever since he was a little kid and had his mother taking off his jacket for him. He loved the fact that no matter what changed in his life, this house and his parents were a constant. The idea that his parents were getting up there in years since they'd waited a bit to have him, and even longer to have Sienna and Violet, was always in the back of his mind, but he did his best to ignore it. He wanted this time with his family, and he would be forever grateful that they were able to spend as much time as they did with Daisy.

Now, if only Sienna and Violet would settle down and have kids, then maybe his parents would get off his back about him being a single father. Of course, the idea of either of his perfect sisters finding a man for themselves made his big-brother radar ping, but he knew it was ridiculous. He wanted them to be happy, but he'd definitely play the overprotective brother when it was needed. That was what he was there for.

"The mushrooms with the cheese?" Sienna asked. "Those are my favorites." She reached out, and Daisy grasped her hand before the two of them skipped into the living room behind his parents.

Mace just shook his head, a smile playing on his face.

"I thought Sienna was the cool and composed one," Violet said, openly laughing. "Look at her skip in those shoes."

Mace had noticed the stilettos and couldn't help but look down at Violet's similar footwear. "You can't skip in yours?"

She elbowed him in the stomach, and he winced.

"You're getting violent in your advanced years, Violent Violet."

"You're an idiot, and sometimes, it's really hard to see why I love you. As for skipping? I value my ankles enough not to try it. Sienna is a braver soul than I am. Though, really, I think I would pay money to see you skip in heels like she just did."

"I don't think they make heels big enough for my feet."

"Drag Queens can find them, I'm sure you can, too. Now, let's get in there before we miss out on all the mushrooms and find Daisy hoarding them all. That little girl is a riot."

He smiled widely. "Yeah, she is. Reminds me of you as a kid, actually."

Violet smiled sweetly. "That's the best thing you could have said. And that also means she will be a total terror when she's a teenager. I cannot wait to see that."

"You're mean. And because you said that, your kid will end up being three-times as bad as you were."

She shuddered. "Okay, that was just cruel."

He kissed the top of her head then took a seat by Sienna since Daisy was kneeling in front of her, studying the mushrooms with a look of deep concentration on her face. She tapped her little lips like she'd been doing more often than not lately—a habit he had a feeling she'd picked up from Adrienne—before pointing to one.

"I think that one is for Aunt Sienna. And this one is for Aunt Violet. And this one, for Grandpa. Then this one...Grandma. And one for me, too."

He leaned down, brushing her hair from her face. "And what about me? Don't I get one?"

She looked over her shoulder and smiled. "Of course, Daddy." She turned back and pointed to the largest mushroom in the dish. "This one's for you. Aunt Adrienne said you were a growing boy and that's why you always eat the rest of her food so she doesn't have to finish it."

Once again, he ignored the laughs and knowing looks from his family as each of them reached for the mushroom Daisy had assigned to them.

"Thank you, Daisy-cakes, this one's perfect." He took a bite of his and blessed the gods for his mother's ability to cook. If he didn't work out as much as he did, these monthly dinners would easily make him gain twenty pounds if he weren't careful.

They finished their mushrooms before heading into the dining room for the rest of the meal, their topics of conversations going from work, to personal, to politics, to...everything. All of them did pretty well with being open about their lives—at least he thought so, but as he was hiding something pretty big, he really had no idea what the others hid. That thought made him pause and look at his sisters, who were very careful about what they told him about their personal lives. However, if he wanted to keep them out of his, he had to be the better man and keep his nose out of their business, as well—for now.

When Daisy nodded off for an afternoon nap on the couch in the den, he tucked her in with the soft throw his mother had knitted and kissed the top of her head before going back into the living room where he figured his family would start to grill him.

He hadn't been wrong.

"What are you going to do, Mace?" his mom asked, wringing her hands. "We can't give her back to that woman."

He sighed, hating the way she called Jeaniene "that woman."

"I don't know, Mom. Right now, legally, I have custody since she's out of the country. However, my lawyer is making sure we get papers filed on our end to set that in stone. We want to make sure we have grounds to get full custody or even complete shared custody where we each get fifty percent when she gets back."

"You'd give her that much?" his mom asked with narrowed eyes.

"She's Daisy's mom," Sienna put in. "Yeah, she's made horrid decisions when it comes to how she treats Mace's relationship with Daisy, but in the end, she's that little girl's mother, and the courts will not only have something to say about that, but so will Daisy."

Mace nodded, his thoughts aligning with Sienna's, but before he could say anything, Violet waded in.

"So, what? She *left* Daisy here with no notice. She doesn't deserve a single moment with that child."

Mace held up his hand because their voices were starting to rise and he didn't want to wake his daughter. "First, we don't know what will happen in the next few months or even years. We'll get through it. But in the end, it's not about what works perfectly for me, but what my daughter needs. And while the way everything happened was *not* in her best interests, Daisy still needs her mom. I'm not going to let her have full custody, though. No matter what happens, I'm going to fight to make sure I get more time in her life than I had before this."

The others started talking over each other as they voiced their opinions, but Mace just leaned back and met his father's gaze. His dad had been silent through it all, but that was because the two of them had already talked in private numerous times about what would need to be done legally. Because, no matter how much any of them wanted to ensure that Daisy was all Mace's, the courts were the ones who ruled, and Jeaniene's family had money and friends in high places. Mace would fight, but in the end, he'd have to wait and see if he even had a chance to continue being the father he wanted—*needed*—to be.

By the time they had finished dessert and Mace buckled a wide-awake Daisy into her car seat, he was emotionally and physically exhausted. He'd worked a half-shift that morning, and had brought Daisy into the shop where Shea had taken her for a girls' morning. He knew he couldn't do that often, though. Somehow, he was not only going to have to find a full-time babysitter or nanny, but he was also going to have to budget for one. He'd been paying child support up until now, and he was waiting for the final paperwork to come in to see what would happen on his ex's end. Everything was so fucking backwards, it wasn't even funny, but no matter what, he had to make sure that everything seemed normal to Daisy. That would always be the most important thing.

"Can we watch a movie?"

He looked down at Daisy and nodded. "Yeah, we have time before bed. Why don't we both get in our jammies first though, and brush our teeth? That way, if we fall asleep, we don't have to wake up to do it."

"Okay!" She skipped off to her bedroom to change, and he just shook his head. He'd give her thirty minutes of the movie—tops—before she passed out. She might have taken a nap and was currently hyper, but it wouldn't last. She usually had an odd amount of high energy right before bed until she zoned out. It had taken him a while to get used to that.

He went to put on his own sleep pants and shirt, though he didn't usually sleep in either. However, he wasn't about to walk around in his boxers with his daughter in the room. His routine had changed dramatically, and he was just going with the flow as much as possible.

They both made it to the living room at the same time, and he tucked her to his side under a shared blanket as they went through their queue for a movie they were both interested in. In other words, he was going to have to sit through another viewing of the Disney movie with the princess with the long hair in the tower. Since he liked the hero, Flynn, and Adrienne liked him, as well, he didn't mind this one as much as some of the others.

Speaking of Adrienne, he'd missed a text from her

asking how he was doing, so he quickly shot her a reply back as the movie started.

Mace: *Sorry I missed your text. Just got home from the parents'. We're sitting down to watch your favorite movie.*

Addi: *Kiss Flynn for me.*

"Is that Aunt Adrienne?" Daisy asked, looking down at his phone.

He nodded. "Yep. She wants us to kiss Flynn for her."

Daisy made little kissing noises with her mouth before patting his phone. "Can she come and watch with us?"

He shook his head. "Not tonight, honey. We're already in our jammies."

She nodded. "Okay. Next time? I love Aunt Adrienne. She's my favorite."

He sucked in a breath, worried that his little girl was starting to fall for his best friend much like he was. But the latter wasn't something he would ever admit aloud, so the only thing he could do was lean down and kiss Daisy's head.

"Maybe."

"Okay, tell her I love her and good night, 'kay?" She snuggled into his side, unaware that she was breaking his heart.

Everything was already too complicated before this,

but Adrienne had been a part of Daisy's life since she was born—a fact that hadn't been lost on or appreciated by Jeaniene. So even though he was going to have to tread far more carefully, he couldn't rip Addi from Daisy's life, no matter how much it might seem better to do so to avoid heartbreak in the end.

Mace: *Daisy says she wants you to watch it with us next time. And you're her favorite.*

Mace: *And she loves you.*

Addi: *Tell her I love her too and next time I'm totally in to watch Flynn Ryder strut his very hot stuff.*

Mace: *You're weird.*

Addi: *And that's what you like most about me. Go cuddle your girl. I'll see you tomorrow.*

Mace didn't text back because the first thing that came to mind wasn't something he could ever say to her, not when so many things were *un*said.

He couldn't fall for Addi, no matter how easy it might be. Because falling was the simple part. It was the landing and living with it that ended up tearing you to shreds.

CHAPTER NINE

No matter how many yoga stretches she did, Adrienne had a feeling her back would ache for weeks after she finished this particular tattoo. Her wrists hurt, and she even had pounding in her temples that didn't seem to want to go away. If she put it all together, it might sound as if she were on the verge of a cold, but she knew that wasn't it. She wasn't getting sick, but she really needed to start sleeping through the night.

Of course, that would probably be easier if she didn't have vivid dreams about Mace and his mouth, his hands, his dick, and all of that other yummy stuff every night. Mace Knight was haunting her dreams, and worse, becoming a very real distraction at work. She hadn't meant for it to happen; yet, somehow, she couldn't stop looking at him when she wasn't working on her tattoos, and her body always knew what part of the shop he was in. It was as if she had a secret antenna only tuned to him, and no matter what she did to ignore it, she could always feel him coming near her.

They were both acting as if nothing had changed when others were around, though. They had always been close, and everyone knew they were best friends, but now, there was a sense of knowing when it came to Mace, and it was hard to put that aside and react like nothing had changed. Whenever they were alone, it was hard to keep her hands off him, but she needed to. They hadn't even defined what they were to each other, even though they kept talking about it and circling around the issue. How could she stay focused on what she needed to do when he was *right there* in all his sexy glory, looking all broody and refined with the white in his hair spreading over the rest of his scalp. That was one sexy, mature-looking daddy of a man right there, and those thoughts just made her want to scream.

Why couldn't she just be normal?

No, instead, she had to become this obsessed weirdo who couldn't stop staring at her best friend. And what was worse, she had *no* idea if he felt the same way about her. And because she couldn't help but focus on that and didn't want to obsess even more, she pushed all those thoughts to the side and kept working. Being in this position alone where she felt as though she were spiraling down the immaturity hole of doom wasn't somewhere she wanted to be.

Ever.

So she looked down at the ink she was working on, ignored her aches and pains, and became whom she wanted to be.

A fucking kickass tattoo artist.

Damn it.

Today, she had a very brave client who wanted a full ribcage tattoo that went all around her back to the other side of her body. While Adrienne had ink on her ribcage that sloped under her breasts, hers didn't reach around her back to become part of one large piece. Hers was mostly smaller pieces put together with the shading of Mace's and Shep's art over time. She still had a lot of open skin for a tattoo artist, but she was picky when it came to what would be on her body for the rest of her life, and only trusted her brother and Mace to get it right. She didn't want tattoos just for the sake of having them, and she knew the old saying of never trusting a tattoo artist with no tattoos wasn't always correct. She had her ink, but most was under her clothes. At least for now.

But for this particular client, her entire back and

sides would be covered by the time Adrienne was done. It would take at least four sessions, five if either of them got too tired or the skin didn't react well during a sitting, and she was honestly freaking excited about it—even if her body hated her at the moment. After this one, she might have to take a nice lower back or upper arm tattoo just to stretch out her sore muscles. God knew the desire for those particular tattoos was in abundance, and she actually loved doing them. Her job was to put her art on someone else's body, permanently. They trusted her with their bodies and something they would wear for the rest of their lives, and that wasn't something she took lightly. Hence why she had three of her favorite and most talented artists working at her shop. Shep, Ryan, and Mace were beyond gifted, and she was blessed to work with them—though, at some point, she'd like to hire another woman when she was able to afford a fifth artist because the testosterone was a little thick.

Her client winced for the fifth time in a row, and Adrienne knew they were done for the day. Jenn was past her endorphin high and was now feeling every stab of the needle on her sore and swollen skin. They'd gotten pretty far on day one and would get back to it soon. For now, though, Jenn would only have the outline of most of the work on one side and her back.

There was no way Adrienne was going to do both sides in one day, not when Jenn was most comfortable lying down during a session. That was just asking for extra pain.

"Okay, hon, we're done for the day. How do you feel?" She sat back and started cleaning off the area, prepping for the bandage Jenn would wear for a few hours.

Jenn didn't stretch since it would probably hurt, but she did let out a relieved breath. "I'm okay. Glad it's over for the day, though. I was doing good for a while, but I think I hit a wall."

Glad she'd read the situation correctly, Adrienne went over aftercare instructions while helping Jenn sit up. Mace brought over some juice and a cookie just in case Jenn's blood sugar was low, and the other woman took it gratefully, her eyes darkening just a bit as she took Mace in.

It took everything within Adrienne not to claim Mace right there, but she knew better than to be an idiot at work. Her best friend was fucking hot, and the idea that countless women constantly checked him out was just something she would have to deal with if she were going to be with him—however *with* him she was.

"Thank you," Jenn purred, and Adrienne barely held in the urge to cross her eyes at the woman. She'd been in pain just a few moments ago, after hours' worth of work, and now she was a sex kitten trying to woo Mace. Of course, she was. "Mace, right?"

Mace smiled his polite smile, not the one that made Adrienne's panties go damp because she knew the dirty words and thoughts behind that expression, and this time, she was the one to hide her own grin. Yep, she had no idea what she was doing in the grand scheme, but Mace was all hers.

The internal alarm that sounded suspiciously like *Star Trek*'s red alert blared in her mind, and she did her best to ignore it. Just because she was calling Mace hers and wanting to lay claim to him didn't mean she was falling for him or anything mistake-worthy like that. All it meant was that she was territorial when it came to those she casually slept with, knowing there were no real promises beyond making sure things didn't get too serious.

And if she kept telling herself that with a straight face, she might actually believe it.

"That's me. Addi's doing fantastic work. Can't wait to see the end result."

Jenn smiled again, this time wiggling off the bench so she could stand next to him. Mace quickly moved forward to help her, and Jenn practically sighed into his hold.

Okay, so this was getting a little annoying, but it wasn't as if Adrienne actually had any right to the jealousy currently swirling in her gut, and Mace wasn't hitting on Jenn. In fact, he was being his normal, professional self, and Adrienne needed to get over herself. Quickly.

"I'd love to show you what it looks like when it's done," Jenn said, leaning into him.

"I'm sure Addi will make that happen. I love seeing her work." Adrienne did her best not to preen at the disappointed look on Jenn's face and went into her pure professional mode as she showed Jenn exactly what needed to happen next and then went to the front desk to schedule the next sitting.

By the time Jenn was gone, Adrienne's headache hadn't abated, and Ryan's client was the only one left since she and Mace had a thirty-minute gap between appointments. She needed to clean up her station, work on the books a bit, and see what was coming up tomorrow since she knew they would only get busier.

Just as she was about to go back to her booth, Mace put his hand on her forearm, stalling her.

"What?" she asked, aware that they weren't the only two in the room. Ryan might be working, but she knew he could turn in their direction at any moment.

"We need to talk." He tugged on her arm, and she moved with him, her stomach clenching.

Nothing good ever came from those words, no matter who said them, and they both knew it. Well, it was good while it lasted, right? It wasn't as if they were serious. She guessed that they would be stopping whatever it was they were doing, so at least she could get back to normal and stop feeling so damn jealous when someone else flirted with Mace. This whole keeping everything inside thing was hurting her brain and making her act so unlike herself. And she wasn't sure she liked this new neurotic person who couldn't stop thinking about how she felt rather than getting things done.

"Ryan, we'll be in the back. Watch the front?" Mace's deep voice brought her out of her thoughts, and her mouth sagged open. What the hell would Ryan think now that the two of them were scurrying off to the storage room? Together. With the door most likely shut.

"No problem," Ryan said, his voice that low drawl of his that made women swoon. Not her, since she had never swooned in her life. But still. Of course, just thinking that, she figured she might just swoon if Mace got all growly and demanding with her, but she was not going to think about that right then. For many reasons, but also because she didn't like how much she'd changed. Ryan gave them a curious look but didn't say anything, and for that, she was grateful. She wasn't sure what she could say anyway.

Adrienne let Mace lead her to the storage room because she knew pulling back and making a scene would only make things worse. But as soon as he had closed the door behind them, she tugged her arm away from his hold and shoved at his chest.

"You don't get to go all caveman on me, dragging me around *my* shop. That's not how any of this works. You *get me*, Knight?"

Mace folded his arms over his chest and narrowed his eyes. "I get you, Addi. And you came with me without complaint. If you had tugged on your arm even the slightest, I'd have let you go. You know I won't hurt you."

Did she? Because she wasn't sure that was the case anymore. Oh, he might not hurt her physically. Or intentionally. But emotionally? She was afraid she'd already gone down the wrong path there, and she might not ever have any hope of finding her way back unscathed.

The thing was, though, she *hadn't* tried to pull away from him. She'd gone freely, his touch comforting even as she was afraid of what the others would see and what was in store. He had her so tied up in knots, she was afraid she'd never untangle them.

"I know that," she said. "But we're at work, Mace. Ryan's probably wondering what we're doing alone in the storage room when there's work to be done. Dragging me off in here wasn't circumspect at all," she added dryly.

Mace crowded her then, her pulse racing as he backed her into the same wall he'd fucked her hard into. She could remember the sensation of her breasts pressed into the coolness of the paint and drywall, and how he'd pumped into her, making her cream all over his dick. She'd almost drenched them, and she knew she wanted to mark him as hers once again.

When he hovered over her, his breath warm against her neck, she arched into him, her body needing him without her knowing.

"Mace. We can't."

He bit down on her neck, and her panties dampened. "I'm not going to fuck you here, not when the shop is open, and anyone could walk in. I didn't lock the door, Addi. Anyone could come in and see me over you. Anyone could smell your need because I *know* you're fucking wet for me right now."

He traced his finger between her legs over the seam of

her jeans, and she bit her lip to hold back a whimper. "You're so hot against my finger. I know if I undid your pants and slid my finger into your cunt, you'd soak my hand, drip down my fingers. But I'm not going to do that."

She pressed her legs together, pinning his hand between her legs as she rocked. When Mace put his other hand on her hip, stilling her, she held back yet another whimper. This man was killing her inch by delicious inch.

"We need to go back out there," she said, trying to find that control she'd once valued.

"We will." He licked her neck over where he'd bitten her, and she knew she'd have to wear her hair down for the rest of the day or anyone who looked would be able to see where he'd marked her. "But first, we need to get something straight."

She met his gaze, pulling away so she could focus. "What?"

"I saw the way you looked at me when Jenn came on to me. She's not you, Addi. It's just you and me, remember? No matter who tries to come between us, it won't matter because it's just the two of us in the end. I've watched these guys come into the shop and drool as they kept their eyes just on your tits as you walked, watching the sway because you're way more than a handful. Which, sidebar, I'm going to need to fuck them at some point. But I digress."

She blinked, holding back a laugh at the serious look on his face as he talked about fucking her boobs. Only Mace Knight.

"You were the one who said you wanted to keep this secret, and I agreed because I don't want to confuse Daisy. So, we're doing what we're doing and keeping it between us. Or, at least, out of her sphere so we don't mess up what we have and what she has with both of us. We're going to have to be careful not to look like we're jealous and want to fuck each other on every flat surface of the shop, though. Think you can do that, Addi?"

"You're so damn confusing." She let her head fall back, ignoring her headache.

"You're not much different," he said. "But, honestly, we were pretty confusing before we started changing things. We're still best friends, Addi, that's not going to change, but you have to know, I'm not going to step out on you. I'm not going to flirt with someone else and be that asshole."

"And I don't understand how I felt jealous." She knew she probably shouldn't be so open and honest about her feelings, but hiding them was only making things worse.

He rubbed his thumb over her cheek. "Yeah. I get that. And it adds a new layer, doesn't it?"

She met his gaze, her chest aching. "We're changing things again, aren't we? I think...I think we need a label. Because without that, it's just making things harder. And for all we say we need to focus on the other things in our lives and not let *this* hurt us, we're spending so much time worrying about what *this* is, that it's getting confusing."

"Friends with benefits doesn't really work, does it?" He frowned, and she blew out a breath.

"No, it doesn't. But we haven't actually gone out on a date."

"We have dinner together at least three times a week." He tugged on her hair, and she let him.

"We did before everything happened. And, honestly, I don't know if I'm ready to go on a capitol-D date and all. I like what we're doing. In bed. It's good for us, I think. At least, stress-wise. But as soon as we get out of bed? I'm so confused."

His lips quirked into a smile, and she rolled her eyes. "I know what you mean." He rested his forehead on hers, and she was afraid if they kept running from what they faced, they'd never find what they needed to. "So, why don't you take some time to think on that. Think about what you want, but know that I'm not going anywhere, Addi. Yeah, I want to keep this separate from Daisy because she's my daughter, my world, but I'm not going to hide completely."

Before she could even think what she could possibly say to that, there was a knock on the door, and the two of them split apart so fast, she was afraid Mace might end up falling on his ass.

"Hey, guys, I think you need to come out here. The cops are here, and they don't look happy."

She stiffened before looking at Mace. The police? What the hell could they want?

And just like that, little problems like what she was doing with Mace went out the window, and the far more important things—her life, her shop, and the person who was out to ruin it—came forward.

She pushed past Mace and made her way out of the closet, passing a stern-looking Ryan. She didn't think that look was for her, but for the two officers who stood in the front area of MIT, their arms folded over their chests and frowns on their faces.

Mace stood at her back, and she knew all thoughts of their personal worries were now out of both of their heads.

Someone was trying to hurt their shop, their second homes. And, sadly, she had a feeling this was only the beginning.

CHAPTER TEN

"They seriously thought you were selling drugs out of the shop?"

Mace's friend Landon sounded incredulous, and he didn't blame the other man for that reaction. Mace couldn't really believe what had gone down the afternoon before either. In fact, he'd been so angry throughout the whole process—and after the cops had left—that he'd taken off after his shift because he needed some space to breathe.

Adrienne had been even angrier than he was, and since they couldn't use their anger to get each other off that night, they'd spent it apart. Frankly, he'd needed time to think anyway. Now, he was out for a beer with Landon and Ryan, trying to relax after several long days and attempting to wrap his head around everything that had happened over the past few weeks—especially last night.

"I thought they were going to cuff you right there," Ryan said, tipping his beer toward Mace. "You walked out behind Adrienne, looking all inked and badass, and I swear both officers twitched as if they were going to reach for their guns."

Mace ran a hand over his face before giving Ryan a look. "It wasn't *that* bad, but having to stand behind Addi as she took the lead wasn't easy."

"She's the owner of the shop, so that makes sense," Landon said, "but having to stand back when your woman is dealing with false accusations, and there's nothing you can do but nod and be by her side...? Rough, man."

Ryan choked on his beer before grinning at Mace. "Your women, eh?"

"She's my friend. My boss. She's not my woman." And that was probably a total lie, but it wasn't as if he could say anything different right then. "But the important thing is, they didn't find any drugs, and were fucking pissed that they had to come in at all. The fact that this is the *second* false call in as many weeks...and then add in the graffiti... We have a serious problem."

Ryan's smile died, and he shook his head. "Someone doesn't like where we opened up the business. And while I'd usually say they can just suck it, they're causing problems."

Mace nodded. "Our walk-in volume isn't as high as it should be for this time of year. Shep and Addi are getting worried."

"You think people are worried about what they're hearing?" Landon asked before pulling out his phone. "How are the reviews online?"

"Good, as far as I can tell, so it's got to just be word of mouth about the calls and issues we've been having." Mace took another drink of his beer then reached for a wing, needing food that was horrible for him to get through his bad mood. Sienna had Daisy tonight since she'd shown up and said she wanted to make a play for the favorite aunt. He hadn't minded, and Daisy was in love with the idea of a sleepover, so he'd let his sister boss him around. It gave him time for dinner and beer with Ryan and Landon—something he hadn't had time for since his daughter came to live with him full-time. Finding that balance wasn't easy, and if it weren't for his family and Adrienne, he knew he wouldn't be able to handle as much as he was.

Ryan peeled at the label on his bottle, frowning. "We give good ink, damn it. Our loyal clients followed us from two different shops and are already on our schedule. And, hell, even Shep has a couple people coming up from New Orleans just for him. He didn't mean for that to happen, but they're making a vacation of it or something. It's pretty awesome. We even have a waiting list for new clients who've heard about us."

"But we're losing some of that initial pull of people who haven't heard of us before and want to get a tattoo closer to their homes rather than driving across town." Mace let out a breath. "And, hell, all this stress on Shep and Addi isn't helping. They risked a lot—as did their cousins up north by increasing their business so much. And I have a feeling we haven't seen the end of whatever this asshole is up to."

"Because it has to be that guy, right?" Landon asked. "It would all be a little too coincidental for it not to be the guy who came in on opening day to threaten you."

"That's what we're thinking."

"By the way, man, I'm sorry I never made it to opening day or even after," Landon put in. "Work's a bit crazy at the moment, but I feel like an asshole."

"You're fine. I have you scheduled for your tattoo, so if you can't make it in before then to see the place, you'll see it in a month when you have time off."

Landon was a broker who worked longer hours than Mace had when he was practically doing overnighters back in the day. And the man was the best at his job. That said, he probably was a little *too* good because his bosses worked him to the bone. Mace was honestly surprised that Landon had been able to join them for dinner and beers. As it was, Shep hadn't been able to make it, and Carter was running late. Mace didn't know Carter all that well, but he'd married a Montgomery woman, and that meant that he was now part of the group—even if he didn't know it yet.

And as if he'd conjured the man out of thin air, Carter walked toward them, a look of exhaustion creeping over his face, but he'd still made it there to hang out with them. The other man worked long hours like Landon, and it was starting to show on both of them. Mace worked his ass off, sure, but he also had a daughter and his health to think about. He wasn't twenty anymore where he could get by on a couple of hours of sleep—but neither were any of the men at this table.

"Hey, Carter." Mace gestured toward the empty seat, and the other man sat down at the table. "Glad you could make it."

Carter smiled, his eyes not looking quite as tired as Mace had first thought. "I wanted to eat dinner with Roxie before I came. I hope that's okay. Between her deadlines coming up and my workers calling in thanks to that flu going around, we haven't been able to eat together most nights this week. But I figured I'd come and hang out for a beer at least."

"See? You're being the good husband," Landon put in. "Us single men over here were forced to eat hot wings that will probably cause heartburn later tonight, but you got good food with your wife. Sounds like the perfect night."

Mace grinned over his beer, and Carter rolled his eyes and explained how neither of them could cook but were learning. "One day, we'll have something better than tuna casserole—the stovetop kind, we're not up to baking it yet." Ryan poured Carter a drink since they'd ordered a pitcher instead of going micro-brew that night. Only Landon had money to spare this month since the rest of them were in the middle of life changes that required them to be slightly more frugal.

"That's love, though. Eating crappy food you make together." Mace lifted his beer up in a toast as he said it, and the others joined in.

Carter rolled his eyes but sipped his beer. "Roxie will end up being a better cook than me, I think. She's determined." There was something else in his voice, but Mace couldn't figure out what it was, and since it wasn't his business, he didn't press.

"Addi's a pretty decent cook, and we all know Thea's a damned fine baker and chef. And I think Shep holds his own, too. Seems the talent didn't trickle down." Mace reached for a wing, slapping Ryan's hand away when the other man tried to filch one from his side. He liked Ryan, considered him a friend, but no one got between him and his wings.

Carter narrowed his eyes at Mace and sipped his beer. "Seems you've been spending a lot of time with my new sister, Adrienne, from what I can see."

Ryan coughed, his grin widening while Landon looked between the three of them, brows raised.

"You and your Addi?" Landon asked, his voice sounding a little too intrigued.

Mace set his drink down and looked at all of the men he called his friends. "She's my best friend." Not a lie. Not quite the truth either. But neither of them were ready for the world to know what they were. And the more important aspect of that was that they didn't actually know what they were to each other yet. Because, for all they praised themselves on talking about their relationship as it was and how they were going to make sure neither of them ever got hurt, he knew they both had their heads in the sand when it came to definitions and feelings.

And maybe, just maybe, that's how they were supposed to make things work for them. At least, for now.

"Yeah? And?" Carter winked as he said it before setting down his beer. He hadn't had more than a few sips, and Mace wondered if the man was going to finish it. All of them were sharing one large pitcher since they all had to drive home, so it wasn't that big of a deal. "Don't tell us, it's fine. But you should know, I saw the sparks between the two of you when I dropped by the shop. And I have a feeling if Roxie and Thea are in the same room as the two of you soon, they'll figure it out."

"If Shep wasn't so focused on the shop and his family, he'd figure it out, too," Ryan put in. "The two of you going off to the storage room together and coming out all red-faced and mussed sort of tipped me off. Just saying."

Landon threw his head back and laughed, the others following suit as Mace didn't confirm or deny what his friends were saying. After all, it wasn't as if he had to. They already knew. Mace had a feeling the cat would officially be out of the bag with the rest of his and Addi's family soon if his friends had anything to do with it—at least by the way they were acting.

Thankfully, the conversation moved onto the Broncos and their slim chances for making the playoffs, and soon, they were stuffed full of wings and mostly water now since they'd finished their one or two beers each.

They said their goodbyes, and because Mace was a glutton for punishment or perhaps because he was addicted to the one woman he shouldn't be, he found himself taking an earlier turn than the one to his house and soon sat parked in front of Adrienne's home. He'd called his sister so he could talk to Daisy before she went to bed, and she said the two of them were camping in Sienna's bedroom, complete with a pillow and blanket fort. His sister had told him to have fun, and had teased him about seeing his woman. He didn't think she knew exactly who his woman was, but he was going to take this time he had.

He hadn't texted or called ahead, and because she usually parked inside her garage, he had no clue if she was actually home or not. This was probably stupid of him, but then again, he was good at making idiotic decisions recently.

He turned off his engine, but before he could get out and walk up to her door, hoping she was home, his phone beeped, signaling that he had a text message.

Addi: *Creeper much?*

He grinned, shaking his head as he replied.

Mace: *If you know I'm out here, then you're the one creeping on me through the window like in that old movie with the birds.*

Addi: *The window movie is not the same as the bird movie, dork.*

Mace: *I'm woefully inept when it comes to classics, it seems. Can I come in and watch some?*

Addi: *...*

Mace: *What?*

Addi: *That's the worst line ever. But come inside, and I'll make you come.*

Addi: *I, uh, mean something eloquent and ladylike that doesn't sound like I'm thinking about your dick.*

Addi: *Because I am.*

Addi: *I mean, I'm not.*

Addi: *I mean, just get in here and let me play with your dick.*

Mace's laugh filled the cab of his truck, and he shook his head, stuffed his phone into his pocket, and headed out into the cold. He locked the truck behind him and hadn't even raised his fist to knock on the door before she had it open and her arms around his neck.

"Hey there, sailor," she teased. He reached down to cup her ass and lifted her into his arms. She wrapped her legs around his waist, and he walked into her house, using his foot to close the door behind them.

"You know I get seasick," he said, turning so he could lock the door before carrying her into the living room.

"Then I'll be gentle." She kissed him then, and he growled, needing her taste more than he needed air.

"It's okay that I'm here, then? That I didn't call?" He didn't want to cross any lines and knew they both needed their own spaces.

She bit his jaw and grinned, her eyes bright. "You never had to before you saw me naked. You don't have to now. Did you have fun with the guys?"

He kissed her behind the ear, loving the way she pressed into him, practically purring in his hold. "Yeah. But Ryan and Carter figured out we're doing our thing, and that means Landon knows. Not sure how long we're going to be able to keep it away from everyone else."

She pulled back, blinking quickly. "I figured Ryan, but Carter?"

"He saw us looking at each other like we wanted to rip each other's clothes off and brought it up tonight."

"Well, then. I guess…I guess we just keep doing our thing and don't lie." She was so still in his arms, he had a feeling if he didn't say the right thing, he'd screw everything up.

"Sounds good to me, Addi. Now, since I'm not as young as I used to be, I'm going to have to set you down on the edge of this couch so I can fuck you hard in a bit. Okay?"

She laughed, doing exactly what he'd wanted her to do, and wiggled from his hold so he could set her down. "Why don't we go into the bedroom? I have that nice, soft mattress. When you're done pounding me into it, I'll let you lay down and relax while I finish you off." She reached between them, rubbing his cock through his jeans, forcing a groan from him. "I *really* miss your dick."

"You say the sweetest things, Addi." He leaned down and kissed her, knowing they were far more than friends at this point, though they wouldn't say it aloud. "The sweetest things."

He followed her into the bedroom and stripped off his jacket so he could lay it on the chair she had by the door. Then he took off his shoes and smiled as she leaned against the end of her bed, watching his movements.

"See something you like?" he asked, his fingers on the bottom edge of his Henley.

She tilted her head as if studying him. "Maybe."

He grinned and slid his shirt up and over his head. "Maybe you'd like it more if I'm closer to you. Say, on top of you as I fuck you into oblivion?"

"Now *you're* saying the sweetest things."

He couldn't hold back any longer. He had to kiss her, had to have his hands on her. They stripped each other out of the rest of their clothes, their bodies coming together as they arched into one another during the kiss. They only let their mouths part to catch their breaths or kiss and lick down each other's bodies. Even then, he knew he had to rein it in, or he'd blow right there on her stomach like a damned teenager instead of the man he was.

Mace licked down her chest, taking one nipple into his mouth and sucking while rolling the other between his fingers. He felt, more than saw, her head drop, and her hair slide down her back, touching the tips of his fingers as he held her so he could take more of her into his mouth. He nibbled her skin, enjoying the way she shivered at his touch before he went to her other breast. He licked and sucked and molded each in his hands. Soon, her nipples were bright red like cherries and so sensitive that she made little noises when he blew on them.

"Mace, I can't take much more."

He moved up and kissed her on the lips, her now sore nipples pressing into his chest. "Then let me make you come."

"I want to make you come, too." She reached between them and cupped his balls, then slid her fingers over his length. He groaned and moved away, a little too close to coming just by sucking on her breasts.

"I need to have my face between your legs in the next thirty seconds, or I'm going to go back to your breasts and make you squirm."

She grinned at him, and he knew she was about to tell him something very naughty and probably something he would totally agree to. "Why don't we do both at the same time? I'll ride your face if you let me suck your dick."

"You come up with the best ideas, Addi." His dick twitched, and he picked her up by her ass and tossed her onto the bed. She bounced and laughed. He'd never thought he could have this much fun during sex. Of course, he hadn't been having sex with his best friend before.

Mace lay on his back, and Addi moved so she could straddle his shoulders. Her wet and hot cunt hovered over his face, and he couldn't help but reach out and grab her ass cheeks to move her down so he could lap her up.

She let out a moan and spread her legs slightly wider so he could have more and take his fill. Then he let out a groan of his own as she practically swallowed him whole. The tip of his cock bumped the back of her throat, and she gave him a hum that went straight to his balls. She stayed there for a moment, moving her throat slightly so it squeezed his dick, and he crossed his eyes before she moved back and let go of him with a wet, sucking noise.

"I'm going to come in about five seconds if you keep being so damn good at that."

She wiggled her hips, and he squeezed her ass harder so she would stop. "Then get to work on eating me out and making me come, and then you'll be so focused on how I taste and feel that you'll last just a little bit longer, old man."

He slapped one cheek hard before running his hand over the new red mark to help ease the sting.

"Bad."

She tossed her hair over her shoulder and winked. "So?" Then she was sucking him again, and he moaned before going back to her pussy. He licked and sucked around her opening, using one finger to play with her clit. She tasted so fucking good that he was pretty sure he'd be addicted to her cunt if he weren't careful. He kept up his ministrations until, finally, her sheath clamped around his two fingers and she came on his face. He was so close to coming as well that he had to pull her off him and slide out from underneath her so he wouldn't lose control too quickly.

He had her on her back in the next instant, one leg up by her ears and the other below him as he teased her entrance.

"Shit. Condom."

"We already talked about this. We are both clean, and I'm on birth control. Now get in me, or I'm going to have to take matters into my own hands. Again. Because I know how to make myself c—"

She didn't get to finish that statement because he speared into her so hard that he was pretty sure his teeth rattled. He waited a moment for her to adjust to his size and then started pounding into her as if there were no tomorrow. Her hips lifted, meeting him thrust for thrust as her hands roamed all over his body as if she couldn't stop touching him.

Knowing he was approaching the point of no return again, he twisted them so she rode him. He cupped her breasts and watched her roll her hips, her body fully seated on his. She was so damn magnificent, he knew he would never get enough of her or the way she came for him. There was nothing better than watching her take control of her sexuality and pull every single orgasm from him.

He reached up and tugged her close so he could capture her lips. Soon, they were both shattering together, their bodies sweat-slick and limp in each other's arms afterwards. She'd wrung him out and had taken every drop of him. And while he knew he needed to move and clean her up, he couldn't help but feel a small bit of wicked satisfaction that she was full-up with him.

He was a sick bastard.

He knew he needed to get ahold of those thoughts because he also knew this wasn't permanent. They weren't going to ruin their friendship, especially with thoughts like the ones he had.

He held her close, helping her descend from her high, and promised himself that come the morning, he'd get his head on straight. Because he couldn't—wouldn't—hurt her, no matter how much he liked her draped on top of him.

He couldn't.

CHAPTER ELEVEN

Livvy slammed into Adrienne's legs, and it took all her power not to fall on her butt thanks to her niece's exuberance.

"You're here!" Livvy screamed, jumping up and down while still holding onto Adrienne.

Adrienne couldn't help but smile and reach down so she could lift the three-year-old into her arms. "Hey, baby girl. I *am* here."

She kissed Livvy's cheek and held her close. She was so in love with her niece and knew she would forever be grateful that Shep and Shea had decided to move up to Colorado Springs. While she knew her brother had done well down in New Orleans and that's how he'd met Shea to begin with, having her family all in one area made everything so much better.

Livvy kissed her on her cheek then on her forehead and chin before wiggling down so she could run to another adult and lavish them with kisses and hugs, as well. She'd been shy at first when she first got to know the Montgomerys, but clearly, that wasn't the case anymore.

"As Livvy announced, you made it," Katherine Montgomery said as she walked up to Adrienne. Her mother was gorgeous and totally didn't look her age. Since she'd had the same color hair as Adrienne for years before she started having to dye it thanks to the silver strands, Adrienne hoped she looked like her mother when she was her age.

Adrienne sank into her mother's hug and sighed. "Yeah, I did. Mace and Ryan are holding down the shop so Shep and I could come and be Montgomerys for the afternoon instead of stressing."

Her mother patted her cheek. "You wouldn't be a Montgomery if you didn't stress over something."

Adrienne rolled her eyes before leaning into her mother's hold. "I did learn from you and Dad, didn't I?"

Her mom laughed before going to help Livvy with something on the other side of the room. The Montgomerys tried to have a family dinner at least once a month. With her brother coming back home, their dinners had been occurring more often than usual—

something she enjoyed even if it was harder to hide some things from them when she needed to. And before the wedding, there had been a lot more get-togethers—for at least the women of the family. Roxie hadn't wanted a huge wedding, but she'd had the small, intimate ceremony of her dreams. At least, that's what Adrienne thought.

Roxie and Carter were off on one side of the room, deep in conversation. The couple went from smiling to frowning at one another often enough that Adrienne had no idea what they could be talking about. But she noticed the way Carter brushed a piece of hair from Roxie's face and smiled down at her as if she were the only person in the world he ever wanted to look at or be with. He was so in love with her sister that Adrienne had to hold back tears when she looked at him as he gazed the way he did at Roxie. She really hoped the couple had decades of loving looks and time together. It was almost enough to make her wonder if she could find love for herself. Of course, she was afraid that she was well on her way to falling when she truly had no business doing so.

Thea stood with Shea, laughing about whatever was on their minds. For some reason, the two had hit it off immediately and become fast friends. Even though Thea already had a best friend in Molly, her sister had opened her arms for Shea without balking. For some reason, Adrienne had figured her sister-in-law would have become faster friends with Roxie since the two shared occupations. But in terms of personalities, Thea and Shea had much more in common than just the similar spellings of their names.

Her dad, William, and Shep manned the grill even as snow began to fall on the frigid afternoon. And while every single woman—minus Livvy—in the room knew how to grill, as well, her father had decided the deck was his domain. He had taught his daughters how to use the Char-Broil for when they had a grill at their own homes, but her dad was very particular about who he let touch his sacred, roaring flames. However, Adrienne had a feeling that Carter would be joining the man at the grill soon. Her father loved the other man like a son, and would probably open his arms to allow Carter near his precious baby grill.

After all, he had let Carter near his precious baby girl.

Adrienne snorted at her lame joke, and was really glad that Mace wasn't around to see her face as she made that horrendous joke. Even in her head. Hell, she was glad he wasn't there for many reasons, particularly so that everyone couldn't see the way she watched him move. If Carter, Ryan, and Shea had been able to figure out even a little bit of what was going on between the two of them, her family would be able to figure it out in a quick minute. She had a feeling the only reason they hadn't already, was because everyone was so focused on their own lives. They hadn't taken a really good look at what she was doing outside of her shop. And for that, she was grateful.

She needed the time to figure out exactly what she wanted when it came to her best friend. And after the last time they had been together when she had fallen apart in his arms so quickly and so completely, she knew she could never go back to the woman she was before she had touched him.

He had touched part of her soul, branded her as his even if she knew it might never be permanent. Things had changed, and hiding what she was doing, what *they* were doing, now seemed wrong. She didn't want to hide her relationship any longer. Because she was afraid that the more time passed where she did, the worse it would be for everyone once the truth came out. She also knew that it could look as if she were ashamed of what she felt for Mace. And that couldn't be farther from the truth. She had a feeling she'd fallen for him long before the first time she'd felt his lips against hers. And that scared her more than anything. Because everything had changed, and if they tried to go back to what they were, she wasn't sure she could find that place anymore. She wasn't sure that place had ever truly existed.

"Is there a reason you're standing here all alone with that sad look on your face?" Roxie leaned into her as she spoke, and Adrienne did her best to pull herself out of her thoughts. She couldn't believe she had once again buried herself in her circular thoughts for so long that she didn't notice when Carter had officially moved over to the grill station and her sister had come to stand beside her. For that matter, she wasn't sure how long Roxie had been watching her.

"Sorry, just thinking about work," she lied and immediately cursed herself for doing so.

"You're going to have to do a better job of lying than that if Mom asks you what's up. And since we're in the middle of the fray, I'll let your lie pass. For now. How about we go get you a drink, because you're empty-handed and standing against the wall with your mouth open like a blowfish."

Adrienne pinched her sister's arm, enjoying how she let out a tiny squeal but laughed. She hadn't pinched that hard, and wouldn't since they were family and loved each other, but sometimes her baby sister was a brat. A smart brat, but still a brat.

"Thanks, I could use a drink." Or four, but who was counting.

She followed Roxie to the kitchen and went to the fridge to get herself something to drink. Her mom had already opened a bottle of white, so she poured herself a glass and topped off her sister's. Instead of going back into the fray, the two of them leaned against the counters and talked like they had when they were younger and stealing snacks when their mother wasn't looking. Of course, their mother had always known, just like she'd always known when they were making faces at each other behind her back. The old adage that mothers had eyes on the backs of their heads had never been truer than with Katherine Montgomery.

"Are you ready for tax season?" Adrienne asked. "As soon as the holidays hit, it's going to start being your busiest time of the year." Usually, during that time, Adrienne didn't get to actually see her sister beyond a few frazzled dinners that their mother somehow made happen. Just the idea of doing taxes made her stomach roll, and her head pound. She wasn't sure how both her sister-in-law and sister ended up with their jobs, but more power to them. Because of them, people like her didn't have to look at all the numbers and start crying daily.

"As ready as I'll ever be. Carter has been through

this with me before, so at least he's prepared for the fact that he'll rarely see me for about four months. Just remind me that I said this in a couple months when I'm ready to pull out my hair because people are constantly showing up with shoeboxes of wrinkled receipts and saying 'good luck.'"

Adrienne winced. "That was one time, and I never did it again. I'd had a hard year and was working even longer hours than you to pay the rent. Now, everything is as color-coded as possible for you."

"Damn straight, it is. I can't have anyone else at the office see me showing up with a shoebox again. The horror, Adrienne. The horror." She winked, and Adrienne rolled her eyes.

"Stop. It wasn't that bad. I know you've seen worse."

"True, but since you're family, I get to rag on you a bit. It was in the contract when each of us was born."

"You're a dork."

"Girls, be nice to each other. Livvy is in the other room, and I don't want her hearing something that she'll end up saying on her own. Be good role models for your niece."

"Sorry, Mom," they both said at once, then looked at one another, smiles threatening to break over their faces. It was as if they were ten again and in trouble for popping wheelies on their bikes with the Thompson boys next door. Those kids had never liked the fact that she and her sisters were far better riders than they were, and Adrienne a daredevil when it had come to stunts. Her mom hadn't been happy about that at all either, but Shep had always secretly taught them everything he knew so they could kick the Thompson boys' butts.

"You'd better be." Her mom smiled as she said it, and her tone wasn't as sharp as it had been when they were kids and in trouble. "Go out on the deck and relax for a bit. Your father turned on the heater before anyone showed up, so it's all nice and toasty. Don't make me waste all that electricity." She winked as she said it before heading back out into the living room to, presumably, play with her granddaughter.

Both Adrienne and Roxie had frozen in place as their mother came out of nowhere to scold them, but now relaxed a bit after she left. After a moment, they went out onto the covered deck with the outdoor heater and relaxed like their mother with her all-knowingness had instructed them.

Seriously, the woman had like ninja skills when it came to finding them doing something they probably shouldn't. It had made being a teenager in the Montgomery house difficult. Shep had been lucky in that he was just old enough when the rest of them had been born that he was able to get away with a little bit more. But as soon as the girls reached their teenage years, her parents had been well trained and ready for whatever trouble they might get into. Needless to say, Adrienne hasn't truly rebelled until after she moved out and buried herself in art.

Mace, thankfully, had wanted to rebel right with her when they met, so she could figure out what kind of alcohol she could have and want, and what kind made her dance on tabletops with only one shot. People always thought it was tequila, but she knew the real answer. Vodka was the Devil's drink. Mace had also been there when she had her first and only cigarette. Apparently, she wasn't destined to become a smoker, and for that she was grateful. That one inhale had made her eyes red and itchy for a week, and she still wanted to cough just thinking about it.

And through it all, she had Mace.

"What is that smile?" Thea asked as she walked out onto the deck with a newly filled wine glass in hand. "You're thinking about that guy of yours, aren't you?"

Adrienne froze, unaware that she'd been smiling while thinking about Mace. "Uh, what?"

Roxie tilted her head, studying Adrienne's face. "You know, that *is* a smile about a man. I saw it before when we were at Brushes With Lushes and you couldn't keep that secret back any longer. So, who is he? I know you said we didn't know him, but does he have a name?"

"What does he do?" Thea asked, taking a seat next to Roxie on the rocker and picking up the conversation. Adrienne sat on the chair next to it, her booted feet up on the outdoor ottoman.

"Is he good in bed?" Roxie added.

"How big is his—?"

Adrienne held up her hands, laughter bubbling up in her throat as she cut off Thea's question. "Oh my God, stop it. Both of you. It's like we're in high school again or something and you're waiting to see what I think about the new boy in study hall."

Thea grinned and took a sip of her wine. "I don't recall asking about length and girth in high school, but not all of us were…seasoned back then."

Adrienne flipped her off. "I had sex *once* in high school, asshole. And never again will I have sex in the back of a Toyota Corolla." She shuddered. "Never. Again."

"So this new man of yours drives something better?" Roxie asked. "Perhaps…a stick?" Her sisters looked at each other and cracked up laughing, and Adrienne just shook her head.

She knew she'd already lied to them once, and since it seemed like many of their other friends already knew about her and Mace—at least the basics since it wasn't as if she actually knew what was going on either—she needed to be up-front with them.

"So, uh, I wasn't exactly truthful before…it's Mace." She shut her mouth as soon as she blurted out his name, out hoped to hell she hadn't just made a mistake. She'd been wishing on that particular hope a lot recently.

Her sisters stopped laughing and stared at her. Roxie's mouth opened and closed like a fish as she tried to figure out what to say as Thea's eyes brightened.

Her middle sister pointed at her and squealed. "I knew it! I fucking knew it!"

Roxie bounced on the rocker, forcing Thea to hold onto the side so she wouldn't fall off, but neither of them seemed to care. "Mace? Your Mace? He's really *your* Mace now, isn't he?"

"Before we get to the burning questions of the century when it comes to you and Mace," Thea began, a twinkle in her eyes, "I'm going to need you to answer the previous questions asked."

"Is he good in bed?" Roxie repeated.

"How big?" Thea grinned. "We already know what

he does and his name, so get on to the good things. I mean, the sex has to be good, right?"

Roxie clasped her hands in front of her chest and did a fair imitation of a regency heroine swooning. "Of course, he is. He's *Mace*."

"Aren't you married?" Adrienne asked dryly. "To the delectably sexy and highly fuckable Carter inside?"

Roxie licked her lips like a cat who had found her canary. "Oh, yes, I'm married to that very sexy man inside who I had a great round of *Sir, May I* before we showed up for dinner, but we're not talking about me and Carter now, are we?"

Sir, May I?

What the hell did Roxie and Carter do in bed? Nope, so not going there. Not even going to let her mind drift in the vicinity of that thought other than possibly asking Mace if he'd like to play. Maybe they'd call it *Ma'am, May I*.

"Okay, that's another grin, but this time, I'm not sure I want to know exactly what you're thinking about." Thea shook her head. "Between the two of you, I'm feeling a little lackluster in the usage of my lady parts area. That may have to change in the new year. Of course, I said that last year and nothing really happened because I've been so focused on the bakery, I don't have time to really care about any dude and his big dick coming in to make me come."

Adrienne snorted, wine going up her nose. She coughed, trying not to cry her makeup down her face. "I can't believe you just said that. How much wine have you had?"

Roxie was choking, as well, but Thea raised her glass in cheers. " I can't always be the sweet and motherly one. Sometimes, a woman just needs the D. But enough about me, Adrienne darling, you didn't answer our questions. Of course, as soon as you do that, I'll have about twenty more for you. So, let's begin this because soon, Mom or one of the guys is going to come out and we're going to have to stop talking about this. Oh my God, does Shep know? He works with you guys, he must know. If he's held this back this whole time, I won't be very happy."

Adrienne held up her hands, stopping Thea before she rambled on any more. "Shep doesn't know. And if you say 'needs the D' again, I might fall off this chair and never recover by the way. But I digress. Shea figured it out, as did Ryan, and maybe even Landon." She looked over at Roxie. "Carter figured it out too, but Mace swore him to secrecy. But he also said, just like Shea, that if their spouses asked them point-blank, they wouldn't lie. Don't get mad at him for keeping it from you. If you're going to get mad, be mad at me, but please don't get mad at all because really...we were just keeping it between ourselves for as long as possible. Now that the cat is out of the bag, I really don't know what will happen."

Roxie frowned but didn't say anything for a moment as Thea just stared between them, a contemplative expression on her face.

"I will jokingly yell at Carter later for daring to keep such a juicy secret from me. Right now, let's get on to that whole you really don't know what's going to happen thing. I also need to know about his dick, because we've mentioned it like five times, and you still won't talk about it. So either it's really sad, and he knows what he's doing with his mouth because you wouldn't stay with him and risk your friendship otherwise, or it's so big that you don't want us to feel jealous. Especially our dear sister over there, who's feeling a little neglected in her nether regions."

Adrienne ran a hand over her face. "Why do we keep using phrases like 'nether regions' and 'lady parts'? This whole conversation is weirding me out."

"Answer the question," Thea demanded. "Because we love Mace, and I always thought he was like an additional Montgomery brother. But, apparently, that is so not what you've been thinking. Unless you sort of were, but then this is a whole part of the conversation I really don't want to have."

Roxie giggled and leaned into Thea, and Adrienne figured they'd talked around the subject enough that she just needed to get on with it.

"First, because I know you won't let me get out of this conversation without talking about it, even a little, here you go." This time, it was Adrienne who grinned like that canary-eating cat. "He's amazing. Hands-down the best sex I've ever had. Biggest…you know what I've ever seen. I'm not going to go into dimensions or measurements because, first, he's mine, and it's something I kind of want to keep to myself. Second, he deserves at least a little bit of privacy even though he probably should've realized that he wasn't going to get any when he became friends with me in the first place."

Her sisters clapped, and she rolled her eyes. Sometimes, it was nice acting as if you weren't an adult with bills to pay and countless lists you needed to check off.

"He makes you happy?" Roxie asked. "Because that's the most important thing."

Adrienne nodded slowly, truly thinking about her answer. "With everything going on right now in the shop and how someone's trying to take it down to do whatever the hell they are planning, he's the one thing that's making me smile."

Roxie sighed happily, but Thea didn't react, as if she knew Adrienne wasn't finished yet. Roxie had always been the dreamer, and though some things had changed in the past year after she married Carter, that part of her remained—if slightly dulled.

Adrienne told them about her first night with Mace and their following nights and how he made her feel. She couldn't help but laugh as the two of them fanned themselves. Adrienne might not have gone into too much detail, but they had been able to guess.

"The thing is, he made me smile before we changed everything. I love you guys, and I love Shep, but I also love the fact that I had connections outside of our family. I know it's the same way with you and Molly, Thea. The idea that I can have these friendships that feel like family outside of the amazing and loving unit we already have, always make me feel more well-rounded. And I didn't realize that really, not until I noticed that Mace needed to rely on me as well as his own family when his ex showed up and dropped off Daisy."

She frowned, trying to get her thoughts in order.

"But now, everything is different. Yet not. We thought we were so smart in talking about each step as I somehow found myself in his arms and not wanting to pull away, yet I don't think there was a way to talk about exactly what we were feeling until we knew what that was. And even now I don't know if I *know*. It's all confusing and exciting and exhilarating and I'm finding myself having these new feelings and fun with my best friend in ways I didn't know I could before this."

"Do you love him?" Thea asked softly.

She met her sisters' gazes and nodded, scaring herself. " I loved him before I thought I was possibly making the worst mistake ever. That love was like a base for what I'm feeling now, and that idea is just scary. I focused on my business and my art for so long that I put aside the idea that I could be with another person. And after everything that happened with him with Daisy's conception and birth and all of the legal problems afterwards with his ex—and even more so now—I don't know what he wants out of what we have. We've done so much to make sure that we're not going to break each other during, that I'm truly afraid what will happen if and when we decided the risk isn't worth it anymore. Because I'm not the same person I was even a month ago, and I think the change is for the better. But I'm really afraid that he's not going to fall for me like I'm already falling for him."

She wiped away a single tear, unaware that she'd let it fall.

"He's your best friend, and I don't think that will

change." Thea spoke slowly as if working through her words. "But I do think if you're truly falling for him like we all think you are in this moment, then maybe you need to state the path you want to take. I'm not saying bare yourself and your feelings. Not yet. Not unless you want to. But maybe you need to make it more than just steamy nights when you can find them. I know you have a little girl to think about, too, but she's already in your life, and you are in hers. But if this is truly what you want, you'll make it happen. There's never been one thing in your life that you haven't been able to grab by the horns, because you throw yourself into things headfirst. I've always admired that about you, and I love you so damn much. So, if you're truly falling for him, take the next step."

Their mother called them in for dinner before anyone else could say anything else, so she hugged her sisters and went inside to enjoy a family meal with people who understood her. And when she got home, she pulled out her phone and took the next step.

Addi: *I think we should go on a date.*

She sucked in a breath, hoping she hadn't made a mistake.

Mace: *Tomorrow good?*

She bit her lip, trying not to smile like an idiot in her own kitchen. It seemed she had her first real date with her best friend tomorrow, and she couldn't help but dance on her feet, her excitement warring with her nerves.

Her sisters were right. If she loved him enough to try and make this work, then she needed to take that next step, that risk. And tomorrow, when she went on a date with Mace that was just about the two of them and not just a friendly meal, she'd put all of herself into it.

Because that's what she did, fear of the future or not.

CHAPTER TWELVE

This was a huge step, at least that's how it felt to Mace. He ran a hand through his hair and wondered if he actually knew what he was doing. Considering that he'd been walking through a murky fog for the past couple of months trying to figure out his game plan, he had a feeling this wouldn't go any better than the other things.

Well, that was just a stupid thing to think. Sure, he kept going at things a little confused and more than a little behind, but it wasn't as if he'd screwed up everything. He was working his ass off at MIT and gaining new clients weekly. Yeah, the walk-ins had decreased ever since the news had spread about the so-called drug deals and sanitation issues, but once they figured out who the man was out to get the shop, they'd be able to bulk up their reputation again. So, while it was really annoying and worrisome that business had taken a hit as it had between the graffiti and those other two major things, he knew they were stronger than whatever else came at them. The whole team was beyond talented, and they had the Montgomerys and their personal reputation backing them. So, whoever thought they had the right to try to hurt them could go fuck themselves.

And as for the most important thing in his life, his daughter? He felt like he was finally finding his footing when it came to raising Daisy on his own. Finding the balance between being a good father and ensuring that Daisy had daily contact with her mother wasn't easy. And a small part of him wanted to cut his ex out of his life forever, not only for what she had done to him in the past, but for what she was doing to her daughter day in and day out in the present. Daisy was still too young to understand exactly what was going on, but she *was* old enough to know that something was different and wasn't the way it was supposed to be.

He was still waiting on the final paperwork and decisions about what would happen in the future with his rights when it came to Daisy, and that unknown made his stomach clench to the point where he was pretty sure he would have to buy stock in antacids.

So, while the monumental legal worries were going on around him, he had to put all of that aside to focus on what was best for his daughter. The two of them had found a rhythm so far that seemed to be working. Because he was able to go into work later since the shop didn't open as early as most nine-to-five jobs did, he could wake up every morning with his baby girl and get her ready for preschool. Then he'd walk her there himself before heading back home to see if he and Adrienne were going to carpool that day. His parents took turns picking Daisy up from school, and they truly loved the fact that they had this time with their granddaughter now.

And though it worried him slightly, Adrienne's role in Daisy's life had changed, as well. His daughter had bonded quickly to the other woman in his life, even before the changes in *their* relationship had happened. His best friend came to his house as much now as she used to, and that meant she saw Daisy more often than not, and his little girl always made sure to say hello when she knew he was texting Adrienne. He knew Adrienne was doing her best not to change the way Daisy saw her, and for that, he was grateful. There was a difference between changing their relationship as a couple and changing the way she was viewed in his daughter's eyes.

And after all of that, he had a feeling he would probably win the award for the most convoluted and circular thought patterns of the day.

His sister Violet would be at the house soon to watch Daisy so he and Adrienne could go on their first official date. He still couldn't believe the two of them hadn't actually been on a date yet. Yes, they had meals together and saw each other every day between work and sleeping together, but he hadn't actually been the man he always thought he was and taken her out in public on a date. Tonight, they would rectify that. The fact that it had been her asking him out rather than the other way around was not lost on him. It had been her saying that she hadn't had sex in over a year while also thinking he was hot at the same time that had led them to sleeping together in the first place. And while he had been the one repeatedly saying that he didn't want to risk their friendship, it had been her saying that they needed to actually talk about the details and what they wanted from each other.

He hadn't been treating her like he should, and he knew he would have to make up for it. She deserved far better than hot sex on lonely nights or in storage closets when they thought nobody was watching. Now that the world had pretty much figured out what the two of them were doing, it was up to them to either make it work or walk away and go back to who they were before so they didn't screw anything up.

So, tonight, he would be the man he should've been all along and treat her like the woman she was. Someone who deserved to be cherished and cared for. And, yes, he also wanted to fuck her hard into oblivion, but the thing was, he knew she wanted to do the same thing right back to him. He was even interested in this whole *Sir* and *Ma'am, May I* thing her sister had apparently brought up. And while they tested that out, he would do his best not to think about Roxie and Carter and whatever the hell they did in the bedroom.

Daisy came into his bedroom right then as he was finishing buttoning up his collared shirt. He wouldn't be wearing a tie or suit jacket since they weren't going anyplace fancy tonight, but he still wanted to look better than his usual raggedy T-shirt and jeans with holes in them.

"What's up, baby girl?" he asked as he turned to her.

"Are you and Aunt Adrienne going out for dinner soon?" Daisy asked. He'd explained to her that he and Addi were going out for a meal, but hadn't been too specific since he wasn't ready to tell Daisy that he and Adrienne were dating.

Since they *were* dating. No more mincing words, even if it made him feel like a teenager again.

"Yep. Your aunt Violet should be here in about twenty minutes, and then Addi and I are headed out. Is that okay?" He didn't want to be one of those parents that let his child dictate how he led his life, he also didn't want to change things up too quickly when she was just finding her footing.

His little girl nodded, her face solemn. "Aunt Sienna said even daddies need time with women they like. Do you like Aunt Addi?"

He was going to kill Sienna. Yes, she'd probably been put in an awkward situation when Daisy had asked her a question about him going out to dinner with Addi, but a little heads-up would've been nice.

"I do." He knelt down in front of Daisy and tapped her on the nose, making her giggle. "She's my best friend."

"Like how I'm best friends with Sarah at school? But she's a girl like Aunt Addi." He'd noticed that she'd started calling her Addi instead of Adrienne more often, and though he knew he needed to be careful, he liked it.

"Yes, like that. And you can be best friends with boys, too." He didn't want to be that dad who was a sexist prick, but he also wasn't really looking forward to her growing up and going through the dating phase—with people of *any* gender.

"I know. Roland is one of my friends, too. He's just not my best friend. But now that I live here, he lives near here too, and that means maybe he'll be my best friend soon. I don't know yet. I have to see."

Mace held back a smile at her words before opening his arms for a hug. Her little arms wrapped around his neck tightly and squeezed, and he stood up so he could carry her into the living room. That's when he noticed that he'd missed a call from Violet since he hadn't known he left his phone in the living room.

She'd left a message, but when he went to listen, he couldn't hear her as it was mostly just static. Worried, he called her, and was relieved when she picked up on the second ring.

"I'm so sorry. Did you get my message?" She spoke fast and, thankfully, this time there wasn't any interference on the call.

"Yes, but I couldn't hear what you said. What's up? Are you on your way?" She should have been well on her way by then if she was going to make it in time, and the fact that she'd called gave him a bad feeling.

"Damn, I knew there was an issue with my phone. I need to get a new one. Anyway, I was halfway there when there was an issue at work. I had to go in. I tried to call, but I didn't get ahold of you. Then I called Mom and Dad, and they were on a date about an hour away—which yay for them but it sucks. Then I called Sienna, but she didn't answer. Only texted me back saying she was finally on a date but that she would cancel right away to come and watch Daisy if you needed her. I didn't really know what to say to her, and now she's waiting on my call. Well actually my text because she said not to call so you can probably tell what kind of date it is."

Mace pinched the bridge of his nose. When Violet got anxious, she rambled, but the fact that she'd gone through all of this after only calling him once and not thinking of the house phone meant that she was truly sorry for not being able to make it down to watch Daisy.

"It's okay. I'll figure something out. Thanks for trying and, hell, thanks for working hard to try and get me out tonight."

"I'm *really* sorry. But, of course, I was doing my best for you. This is a date with you and *Adrienne*. This is like whoa important."

He shook his head, glad that she couldn't see the smile on his face. "It's just a date. Stop freaking out."

"I'll freak out if I want to. Now, I have to go, but

know I'm sorry. And then go hug that baby girl of yours because I'm going to miss our sleepover!"

They said their goodbyes, and he hung up, wondering what the hell he was going to do. Then his doorbell rang, and he figured that he'd just run out of time. Adrienne had said she'd come to his place and pick him up since it was her idea for the date, and since he liked making her smile, he'd agreed.

But now, she was here, and he would either have to cancel their date completely, or find a way to make it work with a hyper four-year-old in the room.

This was so not going the way he'd planned.

When he opened the door, however, he got tongue-tied and found himself unable to speak at the sight of Addi in tights and a slinky black dress under a white coat. How she hadn't slipped on the ice in those shoes, however, was something he would have to ask her later.

"Hey, you," she said, her teeth chattering. "Didn't really think about how much skin is actually showing through thin tights."

He pulled her inside and kissed her temple, closing the door behind her so he wouldn't let out all of his heat. "You look...well...as soon as I come up with words to adequately describe how you look, I'll let you know."

She beamed at him but didn't take off her coat, and

he wasn't sure if he should bother taking it off for her since he was still trying to formulate the next parts of the evening that was now completely off track.

"Well, that's the best way to say hello."

"So, there's a slight change of plans," he said, wincing.

Daisy ran up to Adrienne at that moment and threw herself against her legs. Addi almost fell off her heels, but he gripped her tightly against him, the three of them making quite the trio.

"Be careful, Daisy," Mace warned.

Addi just laughed. "You're like my niece, Livvy. She almost knocked me down yesterday at my family dinner."

"Livvy's three, right? She's younger than me but not by a lot." Daisy looked up at Addi with stars in her eyes, and something inside Mace shifted. He wasn't sure what it was, or if he would ever be able to name it, but he knew he needed to be aware of it.

"Yep. She's only a little younger than you." She looked at Mace quickly before looking down again at Daisy. "Maybe, one day, you'll meet since I think you two would get along great."

"Can we, Daddy? Can I meet Livvy?"

Addi winced, but Mace just nodded. "Sure. We'll try to make that happen." He leaned over and brushed his lips along Addi's temple while Daisy did twirls in the living room in her excitement. Then he leaned over and whispered. "Stop stressing. You're in my life. You're in hers. Even if we're just friends. Okay?"

Her shoulders visibly relaxed, and he hated that he'd made her feel as she had. They were both walking this line and, somehow, they would find a way through it.

"I have bad news, however," he continued. "Daisy, honey, come here for a bit and stop making yourself dizzy."

She blinked, stumbled a bit, then skipped over. "Dizzy Daisy?"

Addie laughed and ran her hand over Daisy's hair. "Dizzy Daisy sounds like a *My Little Pony*."

"She'd be my favorite if she was," Daisy said honestly, and the adults laughed with her.

"Like I was saying, I have some bad news." He cleared his throat as his two girls looked at him. "Violet had to go into work, and the rest of the family is out. That means our date might be a little different. Not canceled, but different."

Addi's eyes looked disappointed for a fraction of a second before she smiled. "So you're saying we get to hang out with little dumpling for dinner?" She hugged Daisy close, and his daughter giggled.

"I'm not a dumpling!"

"You're soft and adorable like one," Addi teased. "And I *love* dumplings. So, Mace, what did you have in mind?"

He looked down at her sexy-as-hell dress as he ran a hand over his head, wishing to hell and back that they'd been able to actually have the date they wanted to—but he guessed they'd make do with what they had.

"Order in?"

Addi rolled her eyes. "Uh, I don't think so. I'm sure you have some prosciutto, pancetta, parmesan cheese, and the makings for some amazing red sauce in your cabinets and fridge. Am I right?"

"Well, of course, I'm like a quarter Italian and that means every once in a while I pretend that I know what I'm doing."

"Okay, then. What do you say we work together and make us a yummy meal? Did you already eat, Daisy?"

His daughter nodded. "But I like other-bacon." She couldn't quite say prosciutto or pancetta so they had taken to calling it *other-bacon*.

"Maybe we'll save you a bite or four," Mace said as he picked up his daughter and hung her upside down. She laughed and wiggled, forcing him to hold her a little bit tighter so he didn't drop her. Addi laughed with them before taking off her shoes and coat. She pulled a soft wrap with armholes out of one of her pockets and slid it over her sexy-as-all-get-out dress. Well, he would forever regret the fact that he couldn't watch her walk around in that dress, but he was glad she looked a little more comfortable in his house.

As he set his daughter down, his best friend took her hand and led them all to start working on dinner. Soon, they were laughing until they cried, eating some amazing food, and starting on the kid-friendly movie until Daisy fell asleep.

And as he met Addi's eyes, he knew that though their date hadn't been exactly what they wanted, perhaps it had been exactly what they needed. What that meant, however, he had no clue. He only knew that having her in his life meant having her in all aspects of his life. He just hoped that if for some reason they couldn't make this work or decided the pitfalls were far too grave, he didn't end up hurting them in the end. Because his little girl had already been through enough, and though he wanted to put his relationship with Adrienne first, he knew he couldn't. But because she was who she was, he knew she would understand...*did* understand.

He just hoped he truly did, too.

CHAPTER THIRTEEN

Adrienne really wanted to get a move on and get to work, but she had a feeling that wasn't going to happen with the headache she was already facing at home. She'd already had to deal with the leaky faucet, a backed-up garbage disposal, and was pretty sure she had almost broken her pinky toe on the edge of her bed. And anyone sane out there knew there was no harsher pain than hitting one's pinky toe on any piece of furniture. She had cursed up a blue streak, and it had all gotten worse from there.

Now, she was running twenty minutes late and having to change shirts because she had spilled her coffee down her front. Thankfully, it had been cold coffee because she had been so busy dealing with household issues that she hadn't actually had a chance to drink it when it was hot. Small mercies and all that.

She'd already had to text Mace and tell him to head to work without her so at least one of them could be on time. Shep had opened, but he couldn't handle the shop by himself when the rest of them all had appointments on the books. Ryan was off that day, but he'd said he wanted to come in on off hours to get some drawings done that he couldn't do at home. She hadn't questioned him on that and, frankly, would be glad to have him around. The shop was a lot more energized when the four of them worked as a group.

However, that meant she had to get in a better mood before she got to work. Because not only did she have three tattoo sessions that day, she also started with a nose piercing appointment. So, now her day was jam-packed, and she just hoped she could handle it all.

Knowing she needed to buck up, she changed her shirt, rolled her shoulders back, and told herself that she was an adult and could do this—no matter how much her pinky toe hurt.

And with all of that, she also had to do her best not to think about where her relationship with Mace was headed. Because that would only activate her headache, and she truly did not have time for that today. She wasn't just falling in love with him. She'd fallen head over heels in love with the man. And with the way he had warned her when they went on their non-date, and how he had included her in his evening with Daisy, she had a feeling things had changed once again. And though she was still nervous, it was an excited nervousness.

But she would have to push all of that to the back of her mind and get to work. She was a freaking adult who owned a business, and she needed to get to work. She hated that she would be late at all, but sometimes, life got in the way of living.

She made her way across the highway to MIT and parked in the parking lot next to Mace's truck. The hairs on the back of her neck rose, and she looked out her side window and gasped.

Shep and Mace were outside the shop, hands on their hips as they stared at the front of the building.

Where someone had broken the Montgomery Ink Too sign into pieces.

Her heart ached, and her hands shook as she took in the physical manifestation of what someone had been trying to do to her business, her second home, a piece of her heart all along: break it.

Methodically, piece-by-piece, someone was trying to tear into what she'd put so much of her life, energy, money, and soul into. Someone had put hateful words where anyone could see. They hadn't cared that children could walk by and see those words, and parents would be forced to have conversations that they might not be ready to have. Because it hadn't just been curse words, it had been horrible, horrible things, which no woman should ever have to see. And now this…parents would always put those conversations in the same place in their mind as her shop. And she couldn't blame them.

They were in a well-respected, family-centric community. And between the new rumors of drugs and uncleanliness added to the destruction of property, she wasn't sure how many more hits to the reputation of her shop, her people, and her soul she could take.

"You're better than this, Adrienne Montgomery." Her voice filled her car, and she took a deep breath, knowing she needed to get through whatever pain was currently digging at her and be the boss she needed to be.

When had she gone from a woman who immediately reacted, to one who needed a moment to get through the grief of what she might lose? She was done with this. Done.

She got out of her car, slammed the door behind her, and stepped towards the shop. At a second glance, the damage didn't look as bad as she had feared. Unless you looked directly at the sign and the subsequent debris on the ground below it, you couldn't really tell that someone had tried to damage her place of business. But she knew, and this was the last fucking straw.

Abby came out of her tea shop just then, a tray of to-go cups of what was most likely hot and delicious tea in her hands.

"Adrienne, I'm so sorry."

At the sound of Abby's voice, the two men standing in front of MIT turned around to look at her. Both had looks showing of a mix of anger and frustration, but they didn't say anything to Adrienne right away. She wasn't sure what was left to say other than cursing and something she probably shouldn't voice it at all.

"What happened?" she asked when she came up on the group.

Abby handed out tea to everyone. And though Adrienne didn't really want anything in her stomach right then and wasn't sure she could handle it at all, she took the cup graciously. As she looked to the left before anyone else could answer, her sister was stomping toward them. Her coat was unbuttoned, she had flour in her hair, and looked like Adrienne felt—as if she were ready to kick ass and take names.

Or, at least, that's how she wanted to feel. She would just have to see if that actually happened.

"We were inside, getting ready for the day since our appointments won't be here for another fifteen minutes," Shep began, "when we heard a loud noise, and the whole building shook. We don't have those fucking cameras up yet, or I would've been able to see who actually threw something at the fucking building. But the cameras don't go up until tomorrow because they were on backorder and the insurance wouldn't let us get anything else."

"Is anyone hurt?" Adrienne asked, trying to take in the situation. Both men shook their heads. "So, that means someone threw something at the sign in broad daylight when people were actually working? What kind of balls do these people have?" She threw her hands up into the air and growled. "If it wasn't for the fact that I put almost everything I have into the shop, I would just say fuck it and find a new place. What the hell is wrong with people? Why can't they just let us live and work in peace?"

She hadn't realized she had shouted that until Mace put his hand on the back of her head and lowered his forehead to hers.

"Breathe, Addi. We called the cops, and they're on their way. We're not going to let this entitled, lowlife scum get away with whatever the hell they think they're doing. We are not going to let them win. The cops will just have to actually take us seriously and do some goddamn detective work to figure out who the hell has it out for MIT. Because it's not just a couple of coincidences anymore. This is beyond vandalism and some petty calls. Someone could've gotten hurt. I almost brought Daisy into the shop, and she could've been walking outside when they threw whatever this was at us. We are going to figure it out. All of it. There's no quitting, Addi. You know as well as I do that Knights and Montgomerys never quit." Then he kissed her right on the mouth in front of her brother, her sister, and her new friend.

Thea did an odd clap before she acted as if she were angry and folded her arms over her chest. Abby smiled as if she'd never seen anything so sweet. While Shep didn't look surprised in the slightest. Apparently, Shea or someone had already spilled the beans, and she honestly didn't care right then. They had far more important matters to worry about than wondering who knew that she and Mace were together. Namely, the two cops who were just pulling into the parking lot. And considering that she'd seen both of these guys before when they came for the graffiti incident, she had a feeling things might just be a little different this time. At least, she hoped to hell they would be.

Adrienne pulled away from Mace, not because of

any looks she may get, but because she needed to remain calm and professional if they were to get any answers as to who thought it was okay to destroy property and screw with MIT. The sad part was, when the cops left, she would have to call her insurance agency, and she already had the number in her most recent calls. The fact that she was practically on a first-name basis with her agent just angered her even more. And she had a bad feeling that without a full report or an actual answer as to why this was happening, her rates would increase. She didn't know how long it would take for her to even replace the sign. She had loved the damn thing, had designed it with her brother and cousins to mimic the one on the original shop up in Denver but with a touch of originality that showed a part of the family down in Colorado Springs. It wasn't as if they couldn't just ask the builder to make another one using the design they already had as a template, but that wasn't the point. It was the principle—for all of this.

By the time the police left, and she and her brother had gotten off the phone with the insurance agent, they had already swept up the debris on the sidewalk so people could easily and safely walk by and into the shop. Their loyal clients who already had appointments for the day showed up and were ready for their tattoos, even with the damage to the outside of the building. They didn't care that the place didn't look as nice as it should have. They only cared about who worked inside and what they provided. The thing was, she knew that wouldn't be the case for every single person. A lot of their initial new business was people seeing their sign —when it was whole—from N. Academy Blvd. and either walking in to see what they could get or making appointments by looking them up. It wouldn't be until much later that they had to rely on that part of their business plan.

As it was, she knew they were already starting to lose money from all of the previous things that had happened. And though they weren't going into the red or having financial issues, it was setting her back on her five-year plan when it came to the shop as a whole.

"Why do you look like you're ready to either bang your head against the wall in front of you or hit the nearest person who comes up behind you. Be aware that I'm asking this a good punching distance away from you, just in case you decide follow through with the latter."

Mace's voice brought Adrienne out of her thoughts, and she turned to see him studying her. His client must have been on her break because he had been working nonstop since they cleaned up the mess outside. Ryan had even shown up to help them put a tarp over the sign once their insurance company said it was okay for them to do so. At the moment, the other man was drawing up a temporary sign to put on top of the tarp. They all knew that wouldn't last long though because it was winter in Colorado and there was bound to be some snow. But for now, everybody was doing his or her part, trying to act as if nothing was wrong and everything would be okay. But from the looks on the officers' faces as they had explained to them what had happened, she didn't know if that would be the case. At least not anytime soon. They had no answers, only more problems. And it was bugging her to no end to feel as though she had no control over the situation.

"Addi?"

"I hate this. I seriously hate this. And I know throwing a tantrum and saying that I hate it does nothing except for annoying everybody and just getting me angrier. I'm just so frustrated." She kept her voice down because she didn't want the two clients in the building to hear her complain, but she knew she needed to get a hold of herself and just calm down. But her heart hadn't stopped racing since she'd first pulled into the parking lot, and the feeling that she couldn't do anything to help her situation just made it all worse.

Mace nodded, running a hand over her cheek. "I get

it, Addi. I didn't like how the officers looked when they left either. But we're not going to back down."

Shep came over then and hugged her. "We're still doing what we love, little sister. And that counts for a lot more than what we let it sometimes."

Ryan came up then, finishing the circle. "We're a team, remember? Fuck the rest of those guys and whatever they think they can do to us."

Adrienne couldn't help but laugh at Ryan's tone. He'd just screamed at her, and though she could still see some of the worry in his eyes, with her guys around her, she had a feeling they could do just about anything.

"We're not going to let these people stop us. We're good about thinking who it could be, and we're going to make them pay." She winced. "Well, you know, legally. Not like a pirate or anything."

Mace smiled. "You know, I kind of like the idea of you as a pirate."

Shep groaned while Ryan laughed. "Just because I'm okay with the two of you dating, doesn't mean I need to see it or hear about it or think about what the hell you might mean about her as a pirate and... God, I really don't even want to finish that thought process."

Mace laughed while Adrienne shook her head. "No walking the plank here."

She closed her eyes, letting out a groan. "Okay, now that we're joking about...whatever the hell we're joking about, I guess this means we're okay?"

"We're not giving up, if that's what you mean," Ryan answered.

"Hell no, we're not giving up," Shep said, frowning. "We're going to figure it out, and we'll give good ink in the middle of it."

"Sounds good to me," Mace said. "We're not giving up," he repeated Shep's words. "We're not going to let them win. But we're going to be safe about it. And speaking of working, my client's almost back so I should go back to my booth."

She leaned into him as he hugged her, and she couldn't help but notice the way her brother narrowed his eyes even as his lips twitched into a smile. "Thanks," she said to all of them. "I needed the pick-me-up."

"We're not letting any of us stay in a funk," Ryan said. "We're in this together."

Shep went back to his booth, while Ryan went back to his to work on the temporary sign. She had to get back to work too since her client would be there in about ten minutes. She just needed to shake off her funk and be the Montgomery she was.

Mace, on the other hand, hugged her close again

and bent down to whisper, "Come over for dinner tonight with us. I think we could all use some time with good food and relaxation. What do you say?"

She couldn't help but smile at his words as she pulled back to look at his face. The fact that he was inviting her to hang out with him and Daisy was a... thing. She couldn't explain it, but she knew that it wasn't just him being her friend. It was him being a part of *them*.

Yes, she was totally in love with Mace Knight, and for the first time, she thought that maybe, just maybe, that was okay.

"Sounds perfect."

"Good." He kissed her on the top of her head then went back to his booth where his client was getting back into the chair.

Adrienne let out a deep breath then rolled her shoulders back and got to work. This whole thing was just an obstacle, just something in her path that she'd kick out of the way when she could.

"Aunt Addi!" Daisy ran into her legs, and Adrienne laughed, this time far more prepared for the little torpedo of energy and love. "You're here!"

"Why don't we go down a decibel or two, Daisy. I think the neighbors can hear you from here." Mace had let Adrienne into the house and now stood beside her, a smile on his face behind his growing beard. He hadn't been shaving daily like he used to, and Adrienne figured this was his winter beard. And since he put coconut oil in it every night, it felt like Heaven when he was between her legs, the scruff of it rubbing along the inner silk of her thighs.

And that was enough of that train of thought.

"Okay, Daddy." Daisy bounced on her feet instead and pulled Adrienne into the living room. "Daddy made chicken bake for dinner. And he bought the crusty bread. You get to eat with us tonight."

Adrienne glanced over at Mace and smiled. "Chicken bake?"

"It's chicken and mushrooms with broccoli all mixed together with like a homemade chicken gravy thing and breadcrumbs on top. It was in my mom's heart-healthy cookbook when I was growing up and was one of her favorite things to make. We don't have a cookbook anymore but we have that recipe. I didn't ask you what you wanted for dinner, but I figured since this is what I was making anyway, and I know what you like, this would be fine."

She smiled. "I remember this recipe. Your mom

made it for us one day when we went over there for dinner and neither of us had any food in the house other than canned green beans. Don't get me wrong, I love me some canned green beans with a little salt and pepper cooked a microwave, but I'm also not nineteen anymore."

"Thank heavens for that," Mace said with a laugh. "You want something to drink?"

"I can get it."

Mace shook his head and looked down to where Daisy was holding Adrienne's hand. "I've got it. White wine okay?"

"Perfect."

Mace went off to get her drink, and she went to sit next to Daisy on the couch. The little girl proceeded to tell her everything about her day and how she'd spent the afternoon with her grandma and grandpa and how she loved spending time with them. After everything the Knights had gone through when it came to getting custody of Daisy, Adrienne would forever be grateful that they all had this time with their precious little girl. She'd even had more time to get to know Daisy, and she had already fallen in love with her even more than she had when she had first held the screaming little infant in the soft blanket. Jeaniene had never been truly happy with Adrienne in Daisy's life, but since the woman had practically abandoned her daughter for a so-called promotion that would apparently *help them all in the end*, Adrienne didn't truly give a rat's ass about what the other woman thought. That probably wasn't the best way to think about Mace's ex, but with everything else going on, she didn't really care. She'd care the next day when she wasn't sitting in her best-friend-slash-lover's living room, talking with his sweet baby girl, about to eat what had to be some truly scrumptious food.

By the time they had eaten and were piled on the couch to watch the latest viewing of *Tangled*, she was full, warm, happy, and once again comparing Mace to Flynn Ryder. She couldn't help it, she had a crush on the Disney character something fierce, and that was just how Mace would have to take her. Imaginary characters and all.

"Stay," Mace whispered, a sleeping Daisy between them.

Her eyes widened, and she looked over at him. Though they had been together for over a month now and were already discussing what to do for Thanksgiving and the rest of the holidays, because of Daisy, they hadn't actually slept a full night together in the same bed. Let alone having her stay over at his place when his daughter was under the same roof. She wasn't sure what it would mean in the long run, but once again, she knew it was the step.

So when she nodded, and he smiled, she leaned over his sleeping daughter and kissed him full on the mouth.

Later that night, they slept tangled under cool sheets and a warm, flannel comforter. They didn't have sex, and he slept in his normal pajamas with her in an old T-shirt of his. But it had been singularly the most romantic and intimate night of her life.

In his arms, she could see a future, even with so many other things going on in her head.

In his arms, she could hope.

CHAPTER FOURTEEN

Mace curled into the woman in front of him and held back a groan. He had to be quiet since his daughter was sleeping down the hall. But since he knew her door was closed as well as his, he may be able to take advantage of exactly what he'd been thinking about when it came to having his best friend in his bed.

Adrienne leaned into his hold as he slowly trailed his hand up under the shirt she wore and cupped her bare breast.

"Mace," she gasped.

He leaned forward and kissed her neck. "Need to be quiet, Addi. I'm going to fuck you, slide my cock between your cheeks, and pump into you from behind, but I'm going to need you to keep your voice down so you don't wake Daisy up. Think you can do that for me?"

She nodded and pressed her plump backside into his raging erection.

"Fuck me," she whispered. And he bit down on her shoulder.

She wiggled into him, and he slid his hand around to gently brush her clit. Her legs immediately parted for him, and his cock slid between them easily, greedily.

"In me."

In answer, he lifted her leg slightly, one hand on her throat, the other on her thigh as he slid into her hot, wet heat. They both moaned, and he took her lips to drown out the sound. They were loud if they wanted to be, and more often than not that was their desire. This morning, however, they had to be quiet. He thrust in and out of her, shallow at first, teasing them both, then full and deep until she was rocking into him as he moved, and they were both panting quietly. She'd reached around and grabbed his ass, forcing him even deeper, and soon, they were moving as one, practically shaking with need.

She came first, her pussy clenching around him, and he soon followed, fully awake now and sated.

He waited until their breathing had slowed down a bit before kissing her shoulder and patting her mound.

"I'm going to slide out. Stay there, and I'll go get a washcloth to clean you up."

She smiled lazily at him, and his heart did that twisting thing he'd been so afraid of. "Okay."

He left her then, in his bed, sticky from his orgasm, and knew if he weren't careful, he'd fall right in love with her.

And the scariest part...he was afraid he already had.

Mace had the morning off while Adrienne had to go into the shop and open with Ryan. He didn't mind since it gave him time to think about what they'd done the night before and that morning, and to get his house in order after a long week of getting into the groove of things with Daisy living there full-time. He needed to start getting better at cleaning up after both of them and teaching Daisy to do some more chores. Sure, she was still a baby in his eyes, but his parents had taught him responsibility early on, and he wanted to make sure that his daughter learned the same things. When Daisy had first moved in, he had been lax in thinking about what she needed to do regarding chores and other things. She was a decently tidy little girl, but her toys had started to spread over the house. Jeaniene's parents had reluctantly packed up—or had hired someone to pack up—Daisy's things at her house, and now her room and the living room were overflowing with little-girl things. And while he loved the fact that she now felt as if she were home rather than just visiting her daddy for the weekend, finding balance wasn't easy.

Daisy was currently organizing her dolls by size so they could be placed on the shelf he had put in that morning once Adrienne left for work. She had already picked up the rest of her toys from her floor and put them in the large trunk that one of Adrienne's cousins had built by hand for her. There were apparently so many Montgomerys being born within a small timeframe that they had made a couple of extras, and Adrienne's parents had shown up with it the day before. They had smiled and had been sure to come when Daisy wasn't around so there wouldn't be any weird questions, but the fact that they had brought a toy chest for his daughter meant something to him. And he knew even if he weren't seeing their daughter, they probably would've brought it anyway. That was just the kind people they were—the kind he wanted Daisy to know. But again, finding that balance where she didn't have to rely on them being the parents of someone he was seeing rather than just amazing people who could be a part of her life was a whole other hurdle.

Mace ran his hand over his face and sighed. He was making everything way too fucking complicated, but the thing was, life *was* convoluted, and his situation was more than most.

His phone rang at that moment, pulling him out of this thoughts, and he quickly answered it, recognizing the number as that of his lawyer. He held back a wince, remembering the amount of the check he had just signed over to the man, but he answered politely anyway. The guy was making sure Daisy could stay in Mace's life beyond the six months his ex was out of the country. He was worth any money it took to make that happen.

"Mace, did I catch you at work?"

"I'm going in later. This morning, Daisy and I are just cleaning up the house."

"Good, good." The man let out a sigh, and Mace stiffened. His lawyer was never one to show any emotion other than the determination to do what was right and necessary to win.

"What's wrong?"

"Nothing's wrong. Or rather, I don't think you're going to think anything is wrong once I tell you what I'm looking at. But, Mace? You're probably going to want to sit down while I explain it."

Mace sat down on the coffee table since he wasn't

sure he could physically make it to the couch based on the tone of the other man's voice. "What is it?"

"She signed over custody, Mace."

He blinked, the roaring in his ears intensifying as each moment passed. He couldn't quite comprehend the meaning of those particular words. His mouth went dry, and he tried to speak, only to find himself unable to say anything.

"Mace? Okay, I'm going to guess you're speechless, so let me explain to you exactly what this means. She is signing over full parental rights to you. She's not even asking for visitation or putting in any addendums for when she moves back to the country. According to her lawyer, who is an ass, by the way, the job is going so well over there, that they are already talking about extending her stay. I don't know what this means for her, and frankly, I don't care other than the fact that she is throwing in the towel and giving Daisy to you full-time, all the time. I don't know if she ever wants to see that little girl again."

Instead of the massive relief he probably should have been feeling to know that the fight was over for him and he would have Daisy in his life the way he'd wanted this whole time, he only felt monumental anger towards the woman who had taken so much from him at the beginning and was now abandoning their daughter as if she were nothing.

"That's not what we went for. We wanted full custody for when she was gone and then talk about partial custody or some form of heavy visitation rights for when she was back. She wasn't supposed to give up everything. She wasn't supposed to abandon her daughter as if she was in the way of her professional aspirations. What the hell am I supposed to tell Daisy?" He had been keeping his voice down, aware that his daughter was in her bedroom with the door open. But she had on music, and he just hoped to hell that she hadn't heard anything he had just said.

What was he supposed to tell her when she asked when was she going to see her mom again? What was he supposed to tell her when two years passed and she was still in his home under his full-time care, and her mom was nowhere to be seen? Why had his ex given up? Was her work so important that she could honestly forget everything she had supposedly fought for at the beginning of Daisy's life?

He couldn't understand it at all, and every time he asked himself another question, he just got angrier. It was all he could do not to throw his phone across the room and scream at the world for the situation Jeaniene had put him in. He'd spent the past month trying to figure out how to be a full-time dad to a little girl who looked at him as if he could carry the world on his shoulders, and now he would have to tell her that everything she'd thought was true was wrong.

He hadn't hated Jeaniene when the first custody agreement had been put into place. He hadn't even hated her when she left Daisy on his doorstep with no warning. But now that he knew she would inevitably break their daughter's heart, yeah, he hated her. And he hated himself for ever being with a woman who could do that.

Adrienne popped into his mind and how he knew she would never do that to someone she loved, or hell, anyone at all, but he quickly pushed those thoughts to the side. He couldn't put her in the same sphere as the thoughts that were currently swirling around in his brain. It wasn't fair to anyone, and frankly, the more he added on to his shoulders right then, the more he knew he might just break and not be the man he needed to be for his daughter.

Jeaniene had done this to him. And he was going to find out why.

"Mace? You still there?"

He let out a curse, remembering that he was still on the phone with the lawyer. He gruffly said, "Yeah."

"I know this is a shock, but it's a win. When and if

she comes back to the country, she will have no rights when it comes to Daisy. If she changes her mind and wants to see her daughter, it will be up to you and how you want to handle her entering Daisy's life again. It's *all* up to you. Come in tomorrow, and we'll go through all the paperwork. But I have to say, Mace, though I know it's going to hurt Daisy, and I don't know how you're going to handle actually telling her, you are not going to lose her because of anything having to do with papers and lawyers. She's your daughter through thick and thin, and now the papers say that, too."

Mace nodded and listened as his lawyer went through more of the legalities that honestly went over his head. He would go through every single paper and ask questions about anything he didn't understand before he signed anything. And, frankly, he was going to make sure his ex did not want to change her mind. Because as much as he wanted Daisy in his life full-time, he didn't want to be the one who stripped away her mother from her life. But, really, Jeaniene was the one doing it to herself. Jeaniene was the one giving up without a fight. It wasn't as if he were fighting to keep her out of Daisy's life completely. No, *she* was doing that.

By the time he'd hung up with his lawyer, his stomach ached, and his head pounded. He knew he needed to tell Daisy soon, or he would let the conversation rot and fester in his mind and in the space between them. But how the hell did he tell her? He figured by now there had to be a few parenting guides on it, but honestly, all he wanted to do was call Addi and ask for her advice. And because that was the first thing that came to mind, he didn't do it. She had so much on her plate, and he was afraid that the more he tangled her up in every aspect of his life, the harder it would be to go back to the way things were when she realized his drama was too much.

That his life was too much for her.

Before he could truly ponder what those thoughts meant, Daisy walked out of her room and came up to where he still sat on the edge of the coffee table.

"What's wrong, Daddy?"

He swallowed hard and knew he needed to do this like it was a bandage. Quick and fast, yet so not painless. His daughter was so bright and caring, she could sometimes get pulled into herself as she thought long and hard about what she needed to do or say in order to work through what she was feeling.

Because he knew he just needed to start and that hiding everything would only hurt them both in the end, he stood up from the coffee table and went to pick her up and hold her close to his chest. She wrapped her little arms around his neck and kissed him softly on the tip of his nose.

His heart melted for her even as it broke. His little girl was everything and so damn strong. So, he would be strong for her. He went to sit on the couch and rested her on his lap so he could meet her eyes as he told her some of what was going on.

"Is it about Mommy?"

He froze, wondering again how he had been part of creating this insightful and wonderful little girl. "Yes, how did you guess that?"

She patted his cheek. "You always get really sad right here when you think about Mommy."

Jesus, he needed to do a better job of hiding that. It didn't matter what else was going on around him, Jeaniene was still Daisy's mom, and he needed to keep from being an ass about it.

He kissed the top of her head so he could gather his thoughts. "Your mom might be staying in Japan for longer than we planned." Why he'd said *we* then he didn't know. There had been no planning when it came to what Jeaniene had done for her job. And he'd had no say when it came to how everything was handled. And now he was going to have to figure out how not to break his daughter's spirit even as he raised her to be a strong, independent woman. Being a single father wasn't easy at the best of times, it wasn't going to get any easier now.

"How long?"

"I don't know, baby. I really don't. But no matter what, it's you and me. We're going to be okay. This is going to be your home from now on, sort of just like we talked about when you first came. You're still going to the same school, and you'll still have the same friends, but you can stay with me for a lot longer. I love you, Daisy, and I love that you're here with me. But it's just the two of us. I know your mommy loves you, but right now she has some adult things for work to do, and that means you and I get more time together."

He knew he was just blowing smoke now, but his daughter wasn't old enough to understand exactly what was going on, and frankly, he wasn't exactly sure himself. How was he supposed to explain the intricacies of whatever the hell was going on in his ex's mind when he had no idea how to even put it into words? He hoped he was doing enough, but in the end, he wouldn't know until something was wrong, and that thought worried him more than he cared to admit.

"I want Mommy. Just the two of us? What about Aunt Addi? Is she going away to Japan, too? Because I don't want to miss her like I miss Mommy. I like her.

And she makes you smile so you like her, too. Don't let her go to Japan with Mommy. Okay? I want Mommy."

Tears fell down her cheeks, and her little body shook as she broke into sobs. He hated himself, and he hated Jeaniene for what she was doing to their daughter. But there was nothing he could do except hold Daisy close and let the sobs finish rocking her body. She was so tiny to have so much within her.

But while all of that was churning, Mace knew he'd made a mistake. Not a little one that could be easily rectified, one that had thrown off the balance of everything that he'd tried to make work. Sorrow filled his gut, but he ignored what he would have to do and hugged Daisy to his chest.

"Just the two of us, baby," he lied hoping he could find the strength to make it true. "Addi is my best friend, so she will always be around, but she's not going to Japan like Mommy. She's not Mommy."

"Okay." And with the resiliency of a child who didn't quite comprehend the delicate emotions running through the air, Daisy went back to her room and turned on her music again.

And Mace quietly broke inside, knowing he was going to have to do the one thing he'd promised he wouldn't do.

Break his best friend's heart. Because he had seen

the start of love in her eyes and felt the same thing running through him. But he couldn't risk Daisy. He couldn't risk hurting her again. Because once the reality of the situation with her mom fully hit her, he was going to have to find some way to help her heal. Whether it was through professional help or just with his family. But he couldn't do anything to make things worse and make Daisy think that Addi was a replacement for Jeaniene. It wasn't fair to any of them.

Dammit.

Mace dropped off Daisy at his parents' house later since it was the weekend and she didn't have school. He went to work and tried to act as if everything was normal and his whole center of being hadn't changed monumentally. Shep would be into work for closing that night since it was his turn, and Ryan had an appointment he couldn't miss, so he'd left as soon as Mace walked in. That left him and Adrienne working side by side as they had countless times before at MIT and their prior shop, as well. She'd given him a weird look when she asked him what was wrong, and he'd lied and said everything was fine, but she didn't question him. Thankfully, they were beyond busy with appointments and walk-ins. It made him think that maybe all of the issues surrounding them hadn't hurt the shop as much as they had thought. But even those worries were in the back of his mind because he was trying to figure out how to let one of the brightest parts of his life go.

He was such an asshole, yet in order to be the father he needed to be, he had to be an even bigger asshole than he already was.

Adrienne would hate him. He knew it. Her family would probably hate him, too. It was going to make working with her and the rest of them almost impossible, yet he would just have to deal with it unless it hurt her too much. Because this was the bed he'd made, and now he had to lay in it. This was why he had tried not to do what they were doing to begin with. He had known that everything was too tangled and complicated, yet he had gone forward anyway, thinking that they could handle anything. He was wrong. So damn wrong. And he needed to figure out a way to make it work again. Because in the end, he had to put Daisy first. She deserved to be first in someone's life. Her mother had already put work and her own personal dreams ahead of what Daisy wanted and needed to survive.

So now, he found himself at home with his best friend standing in his living room, staring at him because he'd been unable to tell her why he'd asked her over while Daisy was still at his parents'. Adrienne had to know that something was off, but he had to do this for Daisy. She was the only thing that could matter, even though so many other things mattered to him, as well. But his daughter had to come first.

"Just tell me, Mace," Adrienne said quickly. "What's wrong?"

"I think it's time we go back to being just friends before we hurt any chances of getting back there," he blurted, his hands fisted at his sides.

Her eyes widened, and she took a step back. "Just like that? No explanations? No, I deserve better than that, Mace. We both do. I know it was a risk when we started down this path, but what changed?"

He needed to be open and honest, and because of that, he told her the truth. Maybe if she saw the *whys* of it, it wouldn't hurt as bad in the end.

"Jeaniene gave up full custody. Not only is she staying in Japan for longer for her job, she also gave up full parental rights. So it's not just custody and visitation. She signed over Daisy to me as if she weren't part of the beginning of our daughter's life at all."

"Are you serious? How could she do that to Daisy? That little girl is like the best little girl ever, and I say that having a niece and cousins who have many amazing babies of their own. What the hell is that woman thinking that she could just walk out of Daisy's life as if these past four years were nothing?"

Some part deep inside of him relished the fact that the first thing that came to Addi's mind was about his daughter's welfare and not the fact that he had just said that things needed to go back to the way they were. But he needed to do what she was doing and focus on Daisy first, and then he would make sure that Adrienne understood what he needed to feel for her—or *not* feel for her.

"I need to make sure that no matter what happens, I'm not going to throw off Daisy's equilibrium any more than it already is."

"And I'm a hindrance to that." She folded her hands over her stomach that hadn't quite hunched in on itself as she spoke. She was such a strong and independent woman, he hated that he was doing this to her. But they had to make this work. He had to find a way to not hurt the two most important females in his life, but he was afraid that each decision he made was just making things worse and worse. He was just grasping at straws at this point, but he needed to make sure that he didn't screw everything up more than it already was.

She didn't pose her last statement as a question, but he answered her anyway.

"I'm not saying that. Not really. She asked if you were going to go away with her mom to Japan, Addi. I can't stand back and watch my daughter go through such turmoil again because she's afraid of losing someone else in her life. She should've been able to trust her mom, but she couldn't. And now I have to hope she can trust me, and because of that, I don't know if I can let her start seeing you as someone other than just a friend in her life. I can't watch my little girl cry again because an adult in her life leaves. I can't put you in that role."

"I was never *in* that role. I know who I am when it comes to Daisy. And the fact that you don't trust me to be a better person than Jeaniene when it comes to that little girl's heart says more about you than it does me. I'm going to let the knowledge that everything in your life has changed so much in the last few weeks help me and let what you said slide. Because that is what you do when you love someone. And, yes, I love you. I didn't mean for it to happen, not like this, but I do. And the fact that you think I could hurt your daughter makes me feel like I don't even know you."

"Addi."

She held up her hand, her shoulders going back, and her gaze meeting his. "Fine. Sign your papers. Sign anything you need. Take your breather and try to get your head on straight as you work on figuring out exactly what your next step will be. When you're done with that, we can talk. Because you don't get to do this. You don't get to throw everything we have away because you're scared. You know as well as I do that there's no way we can go back to the way we were. We're well beyond going back to acting as if our relationship hasn't been changed monumentally. I love you, damn it. And not just as my best friend. Get yourself together, Knight. Because you're better than this. *We* are better than this."

And with that, she walked out of his house and slammed the door behind her. He'd always loved when she was angry because she never held back, and it was sexy as hell. But he knew the anger this time was hiding her pain. Pain he had put her through because he was trying to handle everything the best way he knew how. But he was going about it all wrong. He knew that, and he wasn't sure how to fix it.

He wasn't sure if he *could* fix it.

And he'd just watched his best friend walk out of his house—possibly his life—for the last time.

CHAPTER FIFTEEN

Her mother had always told her that not only did Santa never come to a dirty house, but the new year also couldn't start without a clean home. So when you needed to work through the feelings and thoughts running through your head, cleaning until there wasn't a speck of dust left in your house was the only way to do it.

Adrienne was just about out of cleaning products and elbow grease, and sadly, nowhere near where she needed to be mentally to see Mace again the next morning at work.

Damn it all to hell.

Tears burned the backs of her eyes, and she let them fall, knowing no one was around to see her look weak and *feel*. She could have called her sisters, and had already dodged one call from Thea, but she needed time to think and just be alone for a while.

She'd let herself be happy.

She'd let herself hope.

And look where it had gotten her. Elbow-deep in a toilet with dust and dirt between her boobs. This was not the life she'd signed up for, but it seemed it was the only life fate deemed her worthy of.

She used the back of her arm—the only part not covered in dirt or cleaning products at the moment—to wipe her face so she could see properly. Mace hadn't done this to her, their circumstances had. And she kept reminding herself of that because he was her best friend, damn it, and had been the best lover she'd ever had. She'd thought maybe they would be able to make a go of it. It had felt *right* when it was the three of them in his house, making dinner and laughing at movies. She'd thought she and Daisy were getting along great, and though she knew she never wanted to replace Daisy's mother, she'd thought they had begun to form their own kind of bond on top of the small one they already had. She'd been in Daisy's life since the beginning and now she was afraid she might lose what she had.

She was already losing what she had with Mace, breath by breath, day by day.

She set down the toilet brush and sucked in her lip.

How had she let this happen? Had she truly been so hard-up for sex, for *feelings*, that she'd risked everything she had with him? Because that's what it felt like. That she'd thought she was *so* damn smart that she wouldn't hurt what they had, even though she'd been scared all the time.

But even though he'd broken a part of her, she knew she wouldn't shatter. She hadn't done so when everything happened at her shop, had she? She'd faltered, sure, but anyone would have with all the crap piling on.

But she hadn't shattered.

And she wouldn't break now, even though everything inside her was ready to do so. She'd been strong in front of Mace. Had been honest with him. She *knew* he was scared of hurting Daisy and had to be pissed as hell for what Jeaniene had done. What Adrienne was not happy about, though, was the fact that she had a feeling he was taking his hurt and confusion out on her. Oh, he might not know he was doing it, but that didn't change the result, did it?

He was so afraid of what might happen to his daughter that he was pushing away anything that could possibly disrupt her well-being even without intending to. And while Adrienne understood—she truly did—she was just so damn *angry* that he gave up without a fight. She hadn't, though. She might have walked out of his house the day before because she needed to break down in private, but she'd left him with a promise. Once he got his head out of his ass, she'd be there to watch him grovel.

Not that she needed a big grovel. She just needed her best friend back, damn it.

She sniffed another sob, annoyed with herself. What she really needed was a shower and clothes that didn't have bleach stains on them. Of course, that meant dirtying up one of her newly pristine showers, and she wasn't sure she really wanted to do that right then. That was the problem with doing a deep clean. It got you filthy in the process, and then you didn't want to wash off your grime because you didn't want to dirty the tile.

She was officially a nutcase, and probably needed a glass of wine to make herself feel better. Then she'd call her sisters so she could vent and try to figure out the next steps. Because it wasn't like she was out of Mace's life altogether. He might have said he wanted them to be just friends, but she wasn't so sure that could happen now. However, the two of them worked together, and there was no avoiding him.

And she didn't *want* to avoid him.

She just wanted him to get his act together so they

could figure out what they really wanted rather than what they thought they needed to want.

And that was enough of that line of thoughts. Annoyed with herself once again, she put her cleaning supplies away and finished her list of which ones she needed to replenish since this particular emotional cleaning-fest had depleted most of her stock. Then she preheated her oven so she could make a batch of cookies as soon as she took a shower. Might as well throw flour around her newly sanitized kitchen before she called her sisters and begged them to come over.

Thea and Roxie were her rocks, same as Shep. But she wasn't about to invite her brother over since he'd probably go over to Mace's and punch him or something along those lines. She loved her brother, but he tended to act like a *big brother* who growled at anyone who dared to hurt his precious baby sisters.

Dating or marrying into the Montgomery clan wasn't easy, and so far, only Shea and Carter had figured it out. In the back of her mind, she'd thought *maybe* Mace would be one of the lucky few to pass the Montgomery family entrance test, but perhaps she'd been wrong. Maybe they were better off as friends, and as soon as she licked her wounds, she'd figure that out. At least, she hoped.

Thoughts of Mace and what she might've lost kept spiraling in her mind, but she did her best not to let those thoughts wander or fester because if she repressed it too much, she'd end up paying for it later. She was never one to hide her feelings when it came to most things in her life. That while she had tried to be open with Mace, she'd also been falling in love with him without meaning to, told her that those feelings might have been the most important of all. She wasn't going to give up on him, but she also wasn't going to stand there and let herself be hurt. So whatever came next, it was his turn. His choice. But she wouldn't stand by and let herself be hurt as she waited for an absolution that may never come.

Knowing that she needed to just breathe and let her thoughts wander some more, she set aside the butter sticks to soften and headed into her master bathroom so she could take a quick shower. Of course, she couldn't help but look at where she'd first kissed Mace and where he'd taken her on top of the counter. Her toes curled even as her heart ached, remembering how careful he had been. Mace was always cautious, and perhaps that was their downfall. Because for all of their talk of risk, falling in love and finding a future wasn't safe. Having those feelings wrapped around you, knowing that you could perhaps find safety with another wasn't without risk.

Adrienne had just stripped off her shirt when her phone buzzed on the bathroom counter. Frowning because she recognized the name on the screen and wondered why Mace's sister Violet would be calling her, she answered while standing in her bra and sweatpants in her bathroom. She was still covered in gunk and dirt, but at least she had the smell of bleach away from her face because she had spilled a large drop on her shoulder earlier.

"Hey, Violet? How are you?" She did her best to make her voice sound normal and as if she hadn't been crying most of the day off and on. Like she wasn't desperately in love with Violet's brother even though he had just pushed her away because his ex-girlfriend was a horrible person who apparently only cared about herself.

"Thank God you answered, Adrienne. I called Sienna, and she didn't. Then I called my parents and remembered at the last moment that they were out of town for the weekend. And I can't get ahold of Mace. But he said that might be the case since he was in his lawyer's office all day."

Adrienne straightened, her pulse racing. "What's wrong? Are you okay? Is it Daisy?" She didn't know if Violet was watching the little girl today, but that was the first thing that came to mind.

"I'm watching Daisy, and a migraine came out of nowhere. It would've been fine, and I would've just dealt with it, except Daisy is running a high fever, and I think she needs to go to the doctor because I can't get it down. But I also can't drive right now because I can barely keep my eyes open with the lights on and I feel like throwing up. I have migraine medicine for myself, and I can just ride it out, but I really need someone to take Daisy to the doctor. Can you help?"

Adrienne was already stripping off the rest of her clothes and running into her bedroom so she could put on fresh ones. She may be sweaty and dirty, but at least she'd have on cleaner clothes when she went to pick up Daisy.

"Where are you?" She knew Violet and Sienna lived up in Denver, and though the roads weren't bad, it wouldn't be an easy drive up there.

"I'm at Mace's. I can try to make it work. I just don't want to run us off the road because I can't see."

"I'm on my way. Did you call Daisy's doctor? Or am I heading to the ER?"

"You're a lifesaver. I already called her doctor, and he's expecting her as soon as you can get there. I'm so sorry I can't do it myself, but I really can't drive. This migraine is kicking my ass, and I hate that I'm letting her down. I just really shouldn't be on the roads."

"It's fine. I'll be there in a few. Tell Daisy I'm coming to take care of her."

"I will. Thanks, Adrienne. Truly."

She hung up quickly and ran to the kitchen to turn off the oven. Then she threw the butter back into the fridge and stuffed her feet into her boots and grabbed her keys. She'd probably forgotten a hundred things, but right then, all she could think about was the fact that Daisy was sick, and Violet was scared.

It didn't matter that Mace had tried to quietly push her out of his daughter's life right then. All that mattered was the fact that a little girl was ill, and someone needed to take her to the doctor. The fact that Violet had called her sister, parents, and Mace and then immediately called her warmed her—even if it shouldn't. She had been an honorary Knight for as long as she had been friends with Mace. She wasn't as close to his sisters as she was to him, obviously, but she was still friends with both of them. The fact that Violet had called her meant that she trusted Adrienne to help. She trusted her with Daisy's welfare. And it hurt to think that perhaps Mace didn't.

Growling, she ignored those thoughts since they weren't helping anybody, and quickly got into her car. Hopefully, Violet had the name and address of where she was going, because she hadn't really thought that far ahead, other than getting to Daisy's side immediately.

She had never been more grateful for how close she lived to Mace until that moment. It only took her a few minutes to get to his house, and she parked right behind Violet's car. She practically flew from her own vehicle, not leaving the engine running though she thought about it, and banged on the front door. She had a key, but it honestly hadn't crossed her mind to use it.

Violet opened the door, her eyes covered with her hands and the lights down low. She was pale, pasty, and looked like death warmed over. Adrienne felt for the woman, and if it weren't for the fact that Daisy had a fever and was sick, too, she might have wanted to stay and care for Violet, as well. And who knew, maybe she would come back and do just that. But for now, she really needed to see to the little girl.

"You're here. Daisy is on the couch all wrapped up and ready to go. I have her bag and the address written down for you. I did everything I could, but I really need to go lay down. I'm so sorry I'm out of commission. It came out of nowhere, and I can't get ahold of Mace."

Adrienne brushed past the other woman and took her arm. "Go sit down in an armchair or just lay down. Put your feet up and close your eyes. Thank you for getting everything ready. I'll take care of Daisy. You can trust me."

Violet lowered her hand and frowned. "Of course, I can trust you. I wouldn't trust my niece with just anyone."

That statement hurt her more than it probably should have since the other woman probably had no idea what had happened between Adrienne and Mace the day before.

"Thank you."

Adrienne helped the other woman into the chair then quickly went to Daisy's side. The little girl was sleeping with her hands under her face on the pillow. But Adrienne could see the red in her cheeks and the perspiration on her brow. Then Daisy whimpered, and Adrienne placed her cool hand on the little girl's too-hot cheek.

"Aunt Addi," Daisy whispered. "I want Daddy."

Adrienne's heart broke, and she reached down and gathered the little girl up her arms, careful to grab everything else in her right hand. Then she remembered that she didn't have a car seat and set the little girl back down but hugged her. She really wasn't firing on all cylinders right then because she was freaking out over how warm Mace's daughter felt.

"We are going to make you all better, okay? Just

hang in there for a minute and let me get a few things, and then I'll take you where they're going to make you better."

"I want Daddy."

"I know, baby doll. We will get Daddy, too. We need to get you better first, and then Daddy can come, and you'll be all better." She hoped to hell she wasn't lying.

"Violet? Do you have car seat or booster or whatever in your car?"

The other woman nodded and tried to get out of the chair, but Adrienne waved her off. "Where are your keys? Should I just take your car?"

"It'll take you forever to figure out how to take out the seat and put it in yours. I hate the damn thing. Just take my car."

"Got it." That meant she had to move her car out to the street first because she had parked behind Violet. Everything was getting a little too complicated, but she didn't care. She went through things one by one. First, she moved her car to the street. Then, she picked up Daisy's bag, threw it over her shoulder, put the address to the doctor's office in her phone so she could have her GPS, and gathered Daisy into her arms. The little girl was still sleeping, but she snuggled into Adrienne's hold immediately.

"Thank you," Violet moaned, and Adrienne nodded

at the other woman before leaving her alone in the house, her phone near her in case of another emergency. She hated leaving her there in pain, but there was nothing she could do for Violet at the moment.

Thankfully, Daisy helped Adrienne snap her into the booster seat. She was really behind the times on things like this and would have to get better at it at least for her niece. She wasn't really sure how much of Daisy she would see in the future. Swallowing that hurt, she cupped the little girl's cheek because the coolness of her skin seemed to help, then shut the door and ran around the car to the front seat. Violet had a similar vehicle to Thea, so at least there wasn't a huge learning curve.

She quickly hit go on the GPS and listened to the British man speaking to her in calming tones as he directed her to the doctor's office. Daisy was quiet in the backseat, but Adrienne pulled down the little reflective part of the car's upper dash that she had never used herself so she could see what was going on back there.

It took twenty excruciating minutes to get to the doctor's, and by the end of it, Daisy was crying, and Adrienne's nerves were beyond frayed. She was thinking of crying herself, but held back only because someone needed to be strong in this situation. She gathered up her things and carried Daisy into the office, grateful that the receptionist there stood up immediately.

"Daisy Knight?"

Adrienne had almost forgotten that she had Mace's last name—the one thing Jeaniene had given Mace at the time. She hoped to hell that it was okay HIPAA-wise or whatever legal things needed to be followed that she was the one here with Daisy, but there wasn't another choice at the moment.

"Yes, I'm her father's girlfriend." A lie, but she thought it was better than saying *friend*.

"We know, Ms. Montgomery. Ms. Knight just called and told us you would be bringing her in. As it happens, Mr. Knight already put you on her family list so you can come back with us."

Stunned, she nonetheless followed the other woman to the patient room and stood back as everyone did their thing. Her heart pounded, and she pulled out her phone, then remembered that she probably shouldn't be using it back there.

"I need to try to get ahold of her dad again. Can I use my phone?"

The nurse in the room nodded and pointed at the door. "There's a waiting room right next door where you can use it."

Adrienne really didn't want to leave Daisy by herself, but she also needed to get ahold of Mace.

Her indecisiveness must've shown on her face because the nurse smiled softly. "We will take good care of Daisy. You'll be able to hear us with the door open. Okay?"

"Okay. Sorry."

She went into the waiting room and called Mace. It went straight to voicemail, something so unlike him that it actually started to make her worry. But before she could figure out what she was going to do next, a deep voice filled the air, and her shoulders relaxed even as her belly clenched.

"Lazy Daisy," Mace rumbled from the next room, and tears once again stung the backs of Adrienne's eyes. Was it because of the fact that he was such a caring father, or that hearing his voice reminded her that he'd pushed her away.

It wouldn't matter, though. Not now. She'd made sure Daisy was okay, and now that Mace was there, she figured she would be. She'd ask Violet what happened or even Mace when she saw him the next day at work. There was no use staying there now when her mind and heart weren't ready to see him, weren't ready for him to meet her gaze and speak to her. She should be stronger than this, but she knew she wasn't. Not yet. She needed a few more moments to reconstruct her shields so she became the strong woman she had always thought she was.

She was just walking out the door, careful not to look to the right when Mace's voice hit her again.

"Addi."

She froze but didn't look back.

"Addi." He paused. "Thank you. Just...thank you. I dropped my phone on the way to the lawyer today and it shattered. So I've been out of touch all day and going crazy. When I went home and found Violet like she was, she told me what was going on. I'm so sorry you had to go through all of this. But thank you for helping. Just...thank you."

She swallowed hard but didn't turn back. She wasn't sure if she could.

"No problem, Mace. It was for Daisy. Of course, I helped."

She hadn't meant to sound so passive-aggressive, and she didn't like herself that way. As it was, she could practically *feel* Mace flinch from her words.

Knowing that she needed to face him or she never would, she turned. He was just as sexy as ever, all rumpled and broody, but he'd shaved his beard, making her take a step back.

"I'm sorry, I didn't mean to sound like that," she said quickly. "You shaved."

His mouth quirked up into a semblance of a smile. "I shaved." No explanation, but she wasn't sure she was owed one. How had things gotten so weird, so quickly? "And you don't have to apologize. Not for anything." He let out a breath. "The doctor thinks it's an ear infection and said Daisy should be fine soon. They're just going to keep her for a bit to get the fever down. But, Addi? I'm never going to be able to repay you for taking care of her. I owe you."

She gave him a small smile, knowing it didn't reach her eyes, but she couldn't force it. "I'm glad she'll be okay. And you don't owe me a thing. That's what friends are for."

That's what you do for those you love. But she didn't say that. Instead, she waved awkwardly and turned on her heel, leaving him standing clean-shaven in the hallway, holding her heart as if he didn't know what to do with it. It was okay, she didn't know what to do with it either.

And she was afraid that after today, she might not ever figure it out.

CHAPTER SIXTEEN

There were many times in a man's life when he realized he was an idiot. Mace had been forced to realize that those times were more numerous than he'd originally thought thanks to how he'd reacted three days ago.

Three days ago, he'd broken his best friend's heart.

Three days ago, he'd done a fine job of breaking his heart, too.

Mace slid the razor over his face through the shaving cream again and sighed as he rinsed it off in the sink. He hated shaving, and in the winter, he preferred to keep his beard longer, but he couldn't look at himself in the mirror and see his beard without thinking of her.

He was a sad excuse for a best friend, a sadder

excuse for a man, and he wasn't sure what the hell he was going to do about it. Knowing he couldn't do *anything* about it with shaving cream over half of his face and standing in his bathroom in nothing but a towel, he took his time shaving, trying to get his thoughts in order.

Daisy was sleeping and had been doing so a lot over the past couple of days ever since she'd been diagnosed with an ear infection. Thankfully, her fever had broken quickly, so now she was just sleeping off the worst of the sickness. She should bounce back in the next day and could go back to school. She was already missing her friends and teachers, and by the time she got back, they'd be off for Thanksgiving break. They'd already been invited to his parents' house for the main meal, and he was grateful that he didn't have to cook the whole feast. His sisters would be coming down from Denver and possibly bringing two of their friends who were part of their core group. At least one thing was planned.

He'd taken off work the past two days at Shep's and Adrienne's insistence. They and Ryan had said they would cover for him and make sure that everything was fine at the shop so he could take care of Daisy. He needed to get back to work and make money, of course, but he was glad he'd had this time to not only be with Daisy, but also get his thoughts in order when it came to Addi.

He'd known he made a mistake the moment she walked out of his house. He'd *known* it. Yet he hadn't gone after her because he wasn't sure he deserved her forgiveness for what he'd done. And, frankly, because he was a damn coward.

She had told him she loved him, and he hadn't said a damn thing. He hadn't even known what to think until she was out of the door and his synapses had finally started firing again. He couldn't believe she had bared herself to him like that as he was pushing her away and thinking to protect his family. Only he wasn't protecting Daisy. Not really. Addi hadn't done a single thing to earn the distrust he had for their relationship in general. It wasn't that he didn't trust her. Because God knew he did. More than anything. It was that he wanted to put her into the role of the woman in Daisy's life, and suddenly, he didn't know what to do. But that wasn't on her. It was on him, and what Daisy's mother had done.

Because he'd been so afraid of hurting his daughter again, he'd hurt the one person he was supposed to care for more than anything. The two of them had been through so much in their lives, and he had spent most of his adult life with her at his side, knowing he could rely on her for anything. They weren't just friends. They were best friends. And those weren't just words or titles.

And as soon as he'd kissed her, as soon as he'd made love to her on her bathroom counter, he hadn't been just her friend any longer. If he had made that promise to never hurt her as a friend, then he should have damn well made sure to make that promise when they were something more.

He needed to go to her. He needed to grovel and beg for her to take him back. Because as much as she had said that she would be waiting for him, he didn't know if that would actually be the case. And it wasn't because he didn't trust her words. It was because he wouldn't blame her for walking away from something *she* couldn't trust.

His parents were coming over later to hang with Daisy as he went out and ran errands, but he had a feeling he wouldn't just be going grocery shopping. He knew Adrienne was off that morning before she headed in for a later-than-usual appointment. He was supposed to be working, but Ryan had taken his shift so he could spend some more time with Daisy. He would be forever grateful for his friends, but right now, what he needed to do was figure out what he was going to say to the one woman he cared for more than anything. Maybe that was what he needed to start with. Because she'd said she loved him, and he hadn't said anything back.

Did he love her?

He'd loved her as a friend for ages, but he knew that wasn't the same thing, and nothing like what she had revealed to him while standing in his living room.

The thing was, though, he could see her in his life for more than just a passing moment. He could see her in his daughter's life for the same.

Why couldn't he just say the words? He'd never said them to another person who wasn't in his family, but no one ever mattered that much. Addi had always meant more. She'd always been in his life. She'd always been everything to him. Others had questioned if they could handle each other as just friends with no sexual chemistry and, apparently, there was a slow burn.

When they had been with other people, he knew there hadn't been that connection that they had now. He hadn't felt longing from her, and knew he hadn't felt for her the way he did now when she was with her ex. So maybe time could change feelings.

And as he closed his eyes and tried to think about

what his life would be like without her, he couldn't even comprehend it. Because she was ingrained in every aspect of his life and his heart.

"Fuck. I love her."

He was more than an idiot. He was a deadbeat who deserved more than the lashing he might get when he saw her again. Because he loved her, and he had let her walk out because he was scared. It didn't matter that someone else had scarred him. Addi didn't, and he should have known to trust his feelings when it came to her and not let anything else cloud his thoughts.

And he shouldn't be standing in the middle of his bedroom wearing only his boxer briefs, thinking all of this to himself instead of saying it to her. Because no matter what he thought to himself, unless he gained the courage to say it to her face, it didn't matter. She was the one who'd said it to him first. She had balls of steel, more than he could ever hope to have.

He needed to see her.

He needed her.

It was that simple.

Though nothing was that simple.

He quickly dressed and saw that his parents had arrived to take care of Daisy. He knew he needed to talk to them and his daughter about what might happen, but for now, he needed to focus on Addi. Daisy would always come first for him, but that didn't mean Addi couldn't come in a close second.

His parents gave him curious looks as he practically ran out of the house and to his truck. He didn't know if his best friend was at home, but he figured she would be since she tended to clean when she wasn't feeling up to doing anything but thinking.

Her car wasn't in the driveway when he pulled in, but of course, she could've been parked in the garage like usual. He shut off his engine and took a deep breath, his mind blanking as to what the hell he was going to say to her. He had never been good with words. Never had to be. He'd always put what he felt into his art and how he took care of others around him. He sure as hell hadn't taken care of Addi when he should have, and now he needed to grovel.

If Addi wanted to kick his ass, he would let her. He still hadn't even taken her out in public for a damn date yet because she had been so understanding about how much time he wanted to spend with Daisy. They'd had over a month of hot nights, quick and secret hideaways, and times where they were just together as if it had been the normal thing to do all along.

He was a bastard, and if Adrienne took him back, he would do everything in his power to make sure he was worthy of the love she had so freely given him. And once again, he needed to stop saying this to himself and say it to her. She deserved dates and flowers and grand gestures.

And that was just what she would get today.

He got out of his truck and closed the door behind him. He rang the doorbell and prayed she was inside, then went to his knees. If he was going to grovel, he planned to do it right.

She opened the door and frowned as she looked down. "What are you doing, Mace?"

"I didn't have any jagged glass handy. But if you need me to kneel on that glass in front of you, I will. It'll hurt, but I deserve far more agony than just kneeling on my knees on your porch."

"Mace."

"I'm so damn sorry, Addi. I told you over and over again that you were my best friend and that no matter what, I didn't want to hurt you. And that's the one thing I did…thinking I could protect what I had, I hurt you. You didn't deserve that. You didn't deserve the words I said that cut you like I'm sure they did. I'm so sorry I hurt you. You said you loved me, and I let you walk out of my house. I do trust you. I trust you with everything that I am and everything that I have. I trust you with my daughter's life, and I trust you with *my* life. I shouldn't have put my insecurities on your shoulders. I shouldn't have let what happened with Jeaniene somehow reflect on you. You didn't deserve that. You deserved me telling you exactly what I felt instead of what I was scared of. And I shouldn't have waited so long to come to your door and ask you to take me back."

Tears were falling down her cheeks at this point, and he couldn't help but stand up so he could reach her and wipe them from her face.

"Mace."

"I'm sorry. I'd have gone down on my knees and begged for forgiveness at the shop, or anywhere else you needed me to in public, but I couldn't wait until you were at work. I needed to see you. I should've come before, but I knew you needed your space. You needed time to bake cookies and clean your house to get your thoughts in order. Just like I needed time to get my head out of my ass and realize that I've fallen so far in fucking love with you, Adrienne Montgomery, that I don't know how I could possibly live my life without you. You have been my best friend my entire adult life, and I wish I had known you when we were kids so I could say you've been my rock far longer than that. But I love you. I love the way you smile. I love that you put everything into every single thing you do. I love that you put your family first. I love that you are not afraid of what people think about your job or your ink or your hair or any stupid shit like that. I love that you took a risk in opening a business, and that you trusted me enough to take me along for the ride with you. I love that you took a risk on me. And I love that even when you were hurting, you helped my baby girl. Because that is the woman you are. I should've known that no matter what happened between us, you would always put Daisy ahead of any hurt. Because that is the kind of woman you are. You would have done that for Livvy or any of your siblings. Because that is the strength that flows through your veins. And I am honored to call you my friend. I am honored to call you my lover. I am honored above all that you love me, and I just hope that you will let me love you back."

She was silent for so long, he was afraid he'd either said too much or not enough. He'd told her exactly what he was feeling, yet he still couldn't quite put into words the depth of his need for her.

But before he could go on, she put her fingers to his lips and smiled. "That was the most amazing thing you have ever said to me, Mace Knight. And I have known you long enough that you have said some pretty amazing stuff. Because that is the type of man *you* are. And while I love the fact that you got on your knees to grovel to me, I don't need you to do it again in public. I don't need you to prostrate yourself and make anyone think less of you because of what is going on between us. I love you far more than that. And the fact that you love me? Well, that and you saying you're sorry with your heart in your words makes up for anything you said that night—or didn't say. You grovel good, Knight. Real good."

When she tugged on his arm, he followed her inside, closing the door behind him. He kissed her then, not being able to hold himself back and deny his need for her, for her lips, her taste, just her. When her hands cupped his cheeks, she pulled back and frowned.

"What?" he asked, his voice breathed.

"Why did you shave?"

He kissed her again, biting her lower lip. "Because every time I looked in the mirror and saw my beard, I thought of you. How you loved petting it, how you said it made you want to ride my face. I remembered the way you came on my tongue when my beard scraped up against your inner thighs, and I knew I couldn't look at my beard any longer without thinking of you."

She fanned herself. "Well, then. I guess we'll have to see how well you can go to town with no beard."

He laughed and kissed her harder. "We'll see. If I don't live up to my bearded days, I can always grow it back."

"Because you're a giver."

"Hell yeah, I am."

She led him to the bedroom, and he kissed her, missing her taste. They were gentle at first, slowly stripping each other out of their clothes as they got to know each other's bodies once again. It wasn't as if it had been ages since they had one another, but it had been long enough that Mace wanted to memorize every inch of her again. He'd missed her, damn it, and would never forgive himself for doing what he'd done.

Addi kissed his temple before flicking him. "Stop."

He froze. "What? Did I hurt you?"

She rolled her eyes. They were standing there naked in her room, and she was rolling her eyes at him. This was the Addi he knew and missed. "No, of course not. But you're thinking about what you did and how bad you feel and you're killing the mood. So why don't you go lay on the bed and think of good things—not England, but maybe how sexy I am, please—and I'll have my way with you."

He kissed her hard before moving to lay down on her bed. "Well, since you asked so nicely, but come over here and let me kiss you. I missed you."

Her eyes warmed, and she quickly did as he'd asked. "I missed you, too."

They kissed and licked each other, their hands roaming over each other's bodies. He cupped her breasts, then slid his hand between her legs to find her warm and ready. She slid her hand over his cock, squeezed, then leisurely stroked him as they got to know one another again. And what started out as sweet and slow soon turned into hot and fast.

He was on top of her, sliding into her wet heat as their gazes met. Her mouth parted, and he rocked in and out of her, her pussy clamping down on him as he withdrew as if all parts of her needed him close. As he felt the same way, it all just turned him on even more.

She lifted her hips, meeting him as they came together, and she sighed. "I need you to move faster," she whispered. "I need *you*."

So he moved, increasing the pace until they were panting for one another, the sounds in the room those of sex and need and everything that was part of what he and Addi were. She arched for him, coming hard around his cock, and he followed, filling her up until his body shook and he knew he'd need time to recover before he had her again.

Because he would have her again. Again and again and for as long as she'd have him. Because she was his as he was hers, and he would never forget that. Not again.

"I love you," he whispered. "So damn much."

Tears shone in her eyes, and she cupped his face. "Love you, too, old man."

Then he kissed her again and found that his recovery time was far shorter than he'd thought. His Addi seemed to have that effect on him.

And he would never forget it.

CHAPTER SEVENTEEN

Adrienne threw her head back and arched into Mace as he moved inside her. She was on all fours, her hands gripping the sheets as he thrust in and out of her. He'd already made her come twice at the edge of the bed with his mouth, then once again with him on top of her, then he'd moved so he could play with her ass and rub any soreness away by slowly massaging her even as he fucked her.

Her hair slid down her back, and Mace gripped it, wrapping it around his fist. He was so big, so strong, that he stretched her with each thrust, and she couldn't help but move with him because she knew she gave as good as she got.

When he tugged her back by her hair, she let him move her so her back was to his front and he was fucking her as they knelt together on the bed. He had one hand in her hair, and the other played with her breasts as she reached around her to press him against her even tighter.

"Come, Addi. I'm going to blow, and I need you to clamp down on me. You're so fucking good at that."

She laughed but turned her head so she could kiss him. "Oh, yeah? How close are you?"

"Touch your fucking clit, Addi. Or I'll do it for you. And I know you're already too sensitive there. Do you want to be the one who gives yourself an orgasm on my cock? Or do you want me to torture you with it and drag it out longer so your already tight little nub aches even more?"

She honestly wasn't sure of her answer since both sounded really hot, but because she loved the way he reacted when he watched her play with herself, she slid her hand down over her stomach and just barely brushed her clit. He'd been right, she was so sensitive after so many orgasms in a fifteen-hour period that it almost hurt, but she came right away as if she'd pressed some mythical and magical button that sent her into bliss.

She shouted his name, and he did the same with hers as he filled her up, his cock twitching inside her as he emptied himself. And she'd never found him sexier.

"That's one way to say good morning," Mace teased as they lay facing each other once they'd fallen from their knees.

"The best way. We'll have to make it a routine," she said, her body all heavy and happy.

He leaned forward and captured her lips. "We can do that, Addie mine. We can do that."

And because he was her Mace, her best friend, she believed him.

"So, you and Mace?" her father asked, looking down at his coffee.

"Me and Mace." Adrienne leaned back in her chair, studying her parents as both either looked at her or back down at their coffees after she had told them that, from now on, she and Mace were an item. They were seeing each other, called each other boyfriend and girlfriend, and were talking about the future. There was no mention of marriage or other things like that because they were still in the beginning stages of dating and being in love with one another. There would be time for talk of the future later because she knew they would have one. She'd already told her sisters that she and Mace were officially together. They weren't exactly ecstatic about the fact that he had hurt her, but after she mentioned the whole groveling thing, they had warmed up.

Her parents, on the other hand...she wasn't quite sure how they would react. But she didn't want to hide anything anymore. She had to be open and upfront. Maybe not about what exactly went on behind closed doors, but at least the idea of a commitment and all that jazz. She forced herself not to blush, thinking about exactly what she and Mace did behind said closed doors and then tried not to squirm on her seat since she was still a little tender, but she wasn't quite sure she had succeeded when her mother gave her an eerily knowing look.

And that was enough of that.

"Of course, you are, honey. I've known for a while now." Her mom just grinned, and her dad started to laugh.

"What?" Adrienne asked, setting down her cup. "You already knew? Here I was, ready to stand in front of the Inquisition, and you already knew."

"Of course, we knew, sweetheart," her dad said with a smile. "We're your parents. We know everything. Didn't you learn that when you were a kid?" He winked, and Adrienne put her head in her hands and let out a groan. Thankfully, her parents didn't actually perform the Inquisition, and she was able to enjoy the rest of her coffee before she said goodbye and headed to the shop. She was starting early since she wanted to get a few paperwork things done, but the others wouldn't be in until later.

Of course, her day wouldn't continue to be good because as soon as she parked, she saw the new tags on the front of her building. Someone had put more graffiti all over it, this time using random shapes and letters that didn't form actual words. She wasn't beaten, wasn't sad this time. No tears and no stomach clenches.

No, this time, she was just fucking pissed.

Whoever thought they could run her out of the building was sorely mistaken. MIT would just clean up and keep going. Their business wasn't going to fail because of some asshole. Her people were beyond talented, and everyone who didn't think so could fuck right off. She called the cops and her insurance agent from her car—again—not bothering to stand out in the cold to do so, then texted Mace that he should probably get in and help her clean up. Ryan was out of town, and today was Shep's morning with Livvy since Shea was heading into tax season and needed time to prep.

She took a deep breath and rolled her shoulders back. Shep and Mace had said the action was her putting on her armor so she could kick ass, and right then, they were right. Because fuck the guy who had first come into the shop to belittle their success, and fuck anyone who thought they could take them down.

They obviously didn't know the Montgomerys.

She was out of her car and on her way to the front of the shop when Thea and a man she didn't recognize came out of the doors of Colorado Icing, her sister's bakery. Thea had another splotch of flour in her hair—something that made her adorable even if her sister hated looking a mess at work—and a frown on her face.

"Again?" she said, shaking her head. "Did you call the cops, or should we? Damn it. I'm so annoyed for you."

"I'm pretty annoyed myself." She looked at the man. "Hi, I'm Adrienne, Thea's sister and the owner of this shop over here." She pointed her thumb over her shoulder, trying not to let the sight of all the paint and mess hurt her heart more than it already did. She would *not* back down.

"Oh, this is Dimitri, Adrienne," Thea said, waving her hands. "I thought you'd already met. I'm sorry."

Dimitri was the newly ex-husband of Thea's friend Molly and was also friends with Thea. And, yeah, she had met him before, but it had only been a couple of times and, apparently, she hadn't remembered how hot he was. He was all bearded and mysterious and now that she remembered, had some serious ink that she had admired.

"Oh, yeah, I'm so sorry. Hi, Dimitri. I'm apparently not all there today."

He smiled, inclining his head. "Hi. And, yeah, I remember you, too, though it's been a couple of years. Thea was just filling me in on everything that's been happening with the shop. I know there's probably nothing I can do for you, but do you want me to walk inside with you and check out if there's any other damage?"

She was shaking her head even as he asked. "The door looks fine, so I think it's just like last time with the paint on the front. I'm going to go in and check, though, but I'll be okay. She held up her keys that were between her fingers. "I learned how to walk like this a long time ago."

"Well, let us know if you need us," Dimitri said while Thea came forward and gave her a tight hug.

"Seriously. If you want a donut or a crawler or something, just come on over. I want whoever did this caught."

"I know you do. Me, too. I hope it's not hurting your business." Adrienne had gotten to know each of the owners in the area since they'd started construction over a year ago, but her first priority was always Thea with Abby and her tea shop now following a close second.

"Business is fine," Thea said as she slid her hand through the flour in her hair. "Be safe, and come over later for hot cocoa or something. I miss seeing your face." She hugged her again before whispering, "And I want more Mace details, please."

Adrienne laughed and waved at Dimitri as the two of them went back to the bakery. Adrienne couldn't help but watch as the two walked closely together, talking to one another as if they had done this morning trek countless times before. She wondered what all of *that* was about, but knew it was not only none of her business, but she also had to get into the shop before she froze. She'd wait for the cops there. The other shops wouldn't be open for another hour at least, so it was pretty empty in the area, but she didn't mind. Fewer people to deal with and see the front of her part of the building.

Even as she walked inside, careful not to touch any paint and mess, she couldn't help but wonder if she'd felt some sort of zing when it came to her sister and Dimitri. It was probably just because the two of them were beyond attractive and had chemistry that spoke of what was most likely friendship, but Adrienne could always wonder. Of course, if anything *did* happen, it would be a mess of epic proportions, considering how the two knew each other.

She was just about to turn on the lights and take a look around when a hand covered her mouth. She froze for the barest instant, knowing she'd made a damn stupid mistake.

"I told you to *leave*," the man behind her spat. "You're *ruining* our community. Why couldn't you get that? If destroying your business won't get you out, then I'll have to destroy you."

He ripped at her hair, tugging her to the side and pushing her into the wall. She screamed and turned, punching out with her fist. She got him in the jaw, her key digging into his flesh. He shouted, blood pouring down his face and onto his pristine suit. It was the same man that had come into MIT the first day. The same man who had threatened them, only to seemingly disappear. But if he was here now, maybe he hadn't been all that far away, after all.

"Bitch!"

Adrienne was fast, but he was faster. He grabbed her arm, practically wrenching it from its socket, and she sucked in a breath as pain shot through her system, forcing bile up her throat, coating her tongue.

"Fuck. You." She tore her arm away, a sharp pain ricocheting down her arm, but she ignored it. She had no idea what his problem was, but she *knew* if she didn't get out of there soon, she wouldn't be leaving MIT's doors at all.

"You were supposed to leave," he shouted. "You were supposed to get scared off from the graffiti. The others were supposed to push you out, not want you near them. They weren't supposed to rally around you. Then the cops were supposed to shut you down. So was sanitation. But you kept fucking your way to the top, didn't you? Because that's the only way you got through all those barriers. You slept your way to get what you wanted. Used those hips and tits and that ass of yours, and now you're *ruining* our good name in this part of town."

Adrienne honestly couldn't quite believe what she was hearing. This man wanted MIT gone because it set a poor example or some shit in his mind? Yet he had the audacity to call her those things? To accuse her of using her body?

He was not only seriously deranged, he was also a dangerous asshole with apparently enough power to get at least some people to listen to him—or that's what he thought he had.

The man came at her again, and she ducked, using

her shoulder to get him in the gut. Only she'd used the shoulder he'd hurt, and she retched, the pain almost too much. It wasn't her dominant shoulder, thank God, but she knew she was in trouble if she didn't get out of there.

He came at her again, and she kicked him in the balls, using the pointed toe of her boot. The man went to one knee but still reached out for her. He had her cornered, but if she kicked out again, she might be able to run out of the building and call for help. She'd dropped her phone and keys after the first punch and could have rightly cursed herself for doing so.

He lunged for her again, but the door opened behind them at that instant. Mace was there, fury on his face as he grabbed the stranger into a headlock. She kicked the man in the balls again for good measure, and through the anger in his gaze, she saw pride on Mace's face.

The man went limp in Mace's arms, blood draining from his face from what had to be a tremendous amount of pain—she wouldn't be surprised if he'd busted a ball or something. The asshole deserved it.

Dimitri and Thea were through the doors right after, with Dimitri pushing Thea behind him. Adrienne was damn grateful for that, even though her sister didn't look too happy about it.

Adrienne's adrenaline seemed to have waned completely by then, so she backed up to the wall and slid down, her eyes on Mace.

"Hey. Thanks."

"Jesus Christ."

He was still holding down the man who had tried to destroy her dreams and had hurt her, but all she could think was that she was damn lucky she wasn't alone.

"I fought back."

Mace smiled then, just a small one, but enough that she relaxed marginally. "Yeah. You did."

"But thanks for saving me anyway," she put in. He didn't laugh, but she didn't think he could right then.

"I called the cops," Thea said as she went to her. "They were already on their way for the vandalism, but they're probably coming faster now. And they'll probably need an ambulance." She didn't touch Adrienne but was near enough that it was comforting. Adrienne wasn't sure she could handle being touched right then anyway. Her shoulder and head where he'd pulled at her hair hurt way too damn much.

Dimitri moved to help Mace, and then Abby was inside the building soon after, sitting next to Adrienne. She smelled of tea, while Thea smelled of sugar and chocolate, and Adrienne couldn't imagine a better place to be than in between them—other than Mace's arms.

When the cops came, they took in the scene, and Adrienne knew that things would finally get back to normal—however *normal* things could get with the Montgomerys.

She'd fought back, she reminded herself. She'd won. And Mace being there was just icing on the cake.

"I'm fine, Mom, stop hovering." Adrienne leaned into Mace's side, her good shoulder against his firm skin. Daisy sat on his lap and moved over every once in a while so she could kiss Adrienne's boo-boos. Adrienne had fallen in love with the kid, and she hadn't even processed it, but they'd have time to figure it all out.

"You are in a sling for your shoulder and bruised from where that bastard threw you into the wall." She winced and looked down at Daisy then at her granddaughter, Livvy, who was hiding behind Shea's legs because she was being shy today. "Sorry. He got me all riled up. Don't listen to me when I say bad things, honey."

Daisy just smiled shyly before burrowing into Mace and reaching out to play with Adrienne's hair.

"My shoulder will be fine in a couple weeks. I can

still work some, just not as much as I want to, but there's plenty of admin work I can do while the guys pick up the slack. I didn't tear or break anything, just tweaked it." She wanted to say more, but with Daisy in the room, she was afraid of things that might scare her.

"Hey, Daisy, can you show me your new toy box?" Roxie asked. "I didn't get to see it before you got it. Want to come, too, Livvy?"

Daisy nodded and wiggled off Mace's lap before taking Roxie's hand and leaving the room. Livvy had taken Roxie's other hand, and now it was only adults in the room who could speak freely about what was going on.

"I still can't believe all of this happened," Thea said. "And Dimitri and I feel horrible that we were *right there* and didn't even know until we saw Mace running. I'm so sorry we didn't get there earlier."

"You might have ended up hurt, too. I'm fine. The shop is fine. And Isaac Crawford is behind bars. Or will be once they repair his ruptured testicle."

Her brother, father, and Mace all winced, while Shea, Thea, and her mom did a group high-five. They were as bloodthirsty as she was, and she liked it.

"So, this man was an asshole," Shea began. "A rich asshole, who didn't like the idea of a dirty tattoo shop on his precious, clean street." She spat the words, and Shep wrapped his arm around her shoulder and kissed the top of her head.

"That sounds about right," Mace put in. "Apparently, as he was screaming that his balls were bleeding—ouch by the way—he told the cops everything."

Adrienne growled. "He hired people to damage the building and used his connections to call in to sanitation to try and get us closed down. He never imagined that any respectable tattoo and piercing shop would be cleaner than most buildings in the city. We *have* to be. And ours is damn clean, thank you very much."

"And he called the cops with a fake report on drugs? Or did he hire that out?" Thea asked, her arms wrapped around her middle.

"He did that himself and told the cops that he'd hired out for some things but didn't think it was illegal to be sure there weren't drugs in his nice and family-friendly community." Adrienne rolled her eyes. "Uh, idiot. False claims aren't something you want to deal with, thank you very much."

"And he did all of this because his platform for being a leader in the community was safe and clean and as mundane as you could possibly get," Mace put in. "We didn't know who he was because he's not a leader of *our* community, but apparently, he's a big deal or some shit."

"I don't care how big he is. He got caught, and he might lose a ball. Fuck him." Adrienne gave a quick nod as she said it, and once again, the men in the room winced. They would just have to get used to it because she was damn proud of what she'd done, even if she'd never been so scared in her life.

Okay, she might have been more scared when Daisy was sick, but that was another matter.

The rest of them talked about what they were going to do and how they might have another grand opening party to celebrate the fact that they'd survived Crawford's assholery and would try to remove the taint of what the man and his ideas of *clean* and *safe* had done to the building as a whole.

She listened with half an ear as the people she loved most talked about her dreams and her shop and leaned into Mace even more, knowing she was safe. She had the man she loved, a future she could count on, a family that cared for her, and a business she could call her own.

In the end, Adrienne Montgomery was one lucky woman—sling and all.

"I love you," Mace whispered. "So damn much."

She looked up at him and smiled. "I love you, too."

The resulting *awws* in the room forced her to roll her eyes, and she ducked her head as her family laughed. There were some things that would never change, and her family embarrassing her because they loved her was one of them.

And she wouldn't change it for the world.

CHAPTER EIGHTEEN

"That's it, move back on me, let me see you ride my dick. Take it all in." Mace growled the words softly as Adrienne knelt on all fours in front of him, fucking herself on his cock. She was just so damn sexy when she did this, and he knew they were going to have to wake up in either this position or something similar for a long time to come.

"Hurry up and make me come already, we're going to be late, and I'm shaking."

He grinned at her tone since she was so far on the edge that just one flick over her clit would set her off. So he did just that and watched how she shattered on his cock. Her face went down onto the mattress, her body spent, and he dug his fingers into her ass as he pumped hard, quickly coming himself because he loved the feel of her around his dick so damn much.

When he collapsed beside her, she half-heartedly patted his hip. "Good game, Knight. Good game."

He laughed and kissed her bare shoulder. "We'll go over the highlights later. For now, we need to shower."

"Separately, or we'll really be late."

"And I need to make sure Daisy is up and ready to go, too." They were at his house as they had been more often than not recently. Adrienne had practically moved in. He figured after the holidays, he'd ask her officially. But for now, Daisy was getting used to Addi being around almost all the time, and he loved it.

Jeaniene still called every day to talk to Daisy, but she was firm that the custody arrangements were the right thing for everyone. He wasn't sure how their daughter was going to feel as she grew up, but since he couldn't change things, he'd just make sure Daisy was as healthy and whole as she could be. And Addi was already picking up the slack where he knew he wasn't fully able to. They were a team, and he was damn lucky he realized that before it was too late.

"Sounds like a plan, Knight." She turned and kissed him before skipping toward the bathroom. He just shook his head and grinned. She always got such a boost after morning sex, and went all limp and sleepy after nighttime sex. He never understood how there could be such a difference between the two, but he figured he'd learn since he wanted a lifetime with her to find out.

He wasn't ready to propose, wasn't ready for that kind of change in Daisy's life yet. But he and Addi knew it was a sure thing. They'd even talked about it because the two of them didn't want any more misunderstandings or hurt feelings because they were too afraid of what they might say.

One day, she would be his wife and help him raise Daisy. For now, she was simply his, and he was hers, and Daisy was getting used to the idea of a new woman in her life. Small steps, but strong ones.

By the time the three of them were finally ready for the day, they were indeed late, but his parents hadn't minded. Since today was Thanksgiving, he, Addi, and Daisy were doing two meals: one with his family, and one with hers. He had a feeling since the Knights and the Montgomerys were so close already, one day soon, it would end up as one huge meal. He'd probably be grateful for that. Maybe having his sisters in the same room for long periods of time with Addi's wouldn't be the best thing in the world since they'd probably make plans for dominating the world, but he was just happy everyone got along.

Daisy was chattering away with his parents while eating her turkey, and Mace just smiled, tugging Addi to his side.

"Yeah?" she asked softly.

"Just happy."

She grinned. "Me, too."

"You guys are so cute it's actually a little sickening, but I love it." Violet smiled from the other side of the table and laughed. She and Sienna had come down from Denver since they had the day off work and had brought their two friends they'd known for ages. The four of them had been thick as thieves since college, and Mace was happy that they had each other since his sisters couldn't come down to Colorado Springs every day or weekend like he or they might have liked.

"We try," Addi said, her eyes sparkling. "It takes practice, but our goal is to be so cute, we surpass cute and get right into syrupy."

They all laughed and went about their meals, talking about everything and nothing. Addi's sling had come off a couple of days before, and tomorrow she'd be right back in her booth, tattooing like the crazy talented woman she was. He knew she'd been missing it for the past week or so, but she was healing, and the bruise on her face was almost gone. She'd covered it fully with makeup today so her parents wouldn't worry, but he was just glad it would be faded completely soon.

They finished their first dinner and bundled the three of them up before going over to the Montgomerys for round two. He knew they'd be rolling out the door by the time they were done, but he didn't mind. It was damn good food and company, and that was all that mattered.

"You're here!" Livvy called and ran right up to Daisy. The two of them hugged and jumped around as if they hadn't seen each other in weeks rather than a day. They ran off hand-in-hand to the living room, and Mace shook his head, grinning.

"You know, she used to do that to me. Now, she doesn't even notice when I'm here with Daisy." Addi mock-sniffed, and he kissed the tip of her nose.

"It's okay. I'm glad you're here."

"Dork."

"Yes, you're both dorks, but that's why we love you," Thea said as she took their coats. "I don't know how the two of you are doing two dinners, but more power to you."

"I'm going to have to cut back on potatoes and rolls I think." Addi bit her lip. "Okay, never mind, because I love those, and I'm just going to be a blimp later, and I don't care."

He patted her ass. "Just more for me to handle."

She laughed, and Thea made gagging noises but laughed along, as well.

"Did you bring Molly?" Adrienne asked as they made their way to the family area. Roxie and Carter were talking with Addi's parents, a slight distance between them that Mace didn't understand, but then again, he didn't know them as well as he should have. They all waved them over as Thea answered.

"No, she wanted to stay home and not do anything." Thea shrugged. "I guess I get it. But then I almost invited Dimitri since he's alone too, and hell, he's my friend just like Molly is, but I didn't want to take sides, so now they're both alone and doing whatever, and I'm here with you guys."

Mace hugged her, and she smiled up at him. "Sorry you're having a crappy day."

Thea patted his chest, and Addi raised her eyebrow before winking. "It's okay. I'll be full soon and won't care. I'm just crabby."

"More wine?" Addi asked. "Wine helps."

"Yeah, it does," Thea agreed, and Mace let her go so she could top off her glass.

Addi's dad handed him a beer, and soon everyone was drinking and talking about their lives and the latest Bronco game. His best friend, lover, and future wife leaned into him, and he sighed, knowing that this moment would be one he would always come back to and remember.

He'd run from what he could have and who he could be because he'd been afraid to hurt those he loved, but in the end, he'd gotten everything he'd ever dreamed of.

He had his art, his work, his daughter, his family, and his best friend.

He'd fallen for her long before he truly knew what falling meant.

And when Adrienne Montgomery looked up at him with a promise in her eyes that meant he would still be finding out bits of that secret for years to come, he knew he'd fallen just right.

For his best friend, his partner, and the woman who would one day wear his ring and more of his ink.

***

Coming next...
Thea and Dimitri take a chance in RESTLESS LINK

And Mace's sisters get their own series's tarting with BREAKING WITHOUT YOU

A NOTE FROM CARRIE ANN

Thank you so much for reading **FALLEN INK**. I do hope if you liked this story, that you would please leave a review! Reviews help authors *and* readers.

I'm so honored that your read this book and love the Montgomerys as much as I do! I'm so excited to write more Montgomerys and I cannot wait to dig into Thea's and Roxie's stories. Yes, Roxie is getting her story. Just wait. And in case you missed it, you can find their brother Shep's romance in <u>INK INSPIRED</u>. Up next is <u>RESTLESS INK</u> and oh my, just wait until you see what Thea and this new man Dimitri are up to!

And if you loved Mace's sisters, don't worry, they're getting their own series with the <u>Fractured Connections</u> series, starting with <u>BREAKING WITHOUT YOU</u>!

Montgomery Ink: Colorado Springs
- Book 1: Fallen Ink
- Book 2: Restless Ink
- Book 2.5: Ashes to Ink
- Book 3: Jagged Ink
- Book 3.5: Ink by Numbers

If you want to make sure you know what's coming next from me, you can sign up for my newsletter at www.CarrieAnnRyan.com; follow me on twitter at @CarrieAnnRyan, or like my Facebook page. I also have a Facebook Fan Club where we have trivia, chats, and other goodies. You guys are the reason I get to do what I do and I thank you.

Make sure you're signed up for my MAILING LIST so you can know when the next releases are available as well as find giveaways and FREE READS.

Happy Reading!

ALSO FROM CARRIE ANN RYAN

The Montgomery Ink Legacy Series:
Book 1: Bittersweet Promises (Leif & Brooke)
Book 2: At First Meet (Nick & Lake)
Book 2.5: Happily Ever Never (May & Leo)
Book 3: Longtime Crush (Sebastian & Raven)
Book 4: Best Friend Temptation (Noah, Ford, and Greer)
Book 4.5: Happily Ever Maybe (Jennifer & Gus)
Book 5: Last First Kiss (Daisy & Hugh)
Book 6: His Second Chance (Kane & Phoebe)
Book 7: One Night with You (Kingston & Claire)
Book 8: Accidentally Forever (Crew & Aria)
Book 9: Last Chance Seduction (Lexington & Mercy)
Book 10: Kiss Me Forever (Brooklyn & Reece)
Book 11: His Guilty Pleasure (Dash & Aly)

ALSO FROM CARRIE ANN RYAN

Book 12: Maybe it's You (Riley & Gage)

The Cage Family
Book 1: The Forever Rule (Aston & Blakely)
Book 2: An Unexpected Everything (Isabella & Weston)
Book 3: If You Were Mine (Dorian & Harper)
Book 4: One Quick Obsession (Hudson & Scarlett)
Book 5: Pretend it's Forever (Sophia & Carson)
Book 6: Wish it Were You (Flynn & Luna)

Ashford Creek
Book 1: Legacy (Callum & Felicity)
Book 2: Crossroads (Bodhi & Kiera)
Book 3: Westward (Atlas & Elizabeth)
Book 4: Patience (Teagan & Rush)

Clover Lake
Book 1: Always a Fake Bridesmaid (Livvy & Ewan)
Book 2: Accidental Runaway Groom (Jamie & Sharp)
Book 3: His Practically Fake Proposal (Galen & Addy)

The Wilder Brothers Series:
Book 1: One Way Back to Me (Eli & Alexis)

Book 2: Always the One for Me (Evan & Kendall)
Book 3: The Path to You (Everett & Bethany)
Book 4: Coming Home for Us (Elijah & Maddie)
Book 5: Stay Here With Me (East & Lark)
Book 6: Finding the Road to Us (Elliot, Trace, and Sidney)
Book 7: Moments for You (Ridge & Aurora)
Book 7.5: A Wilder Wedding (Amos & Naomi)
Book 8: Forever For Us (Wyatt & Ava)
Book 9: Pieces of Me (Gabriel & Briar)
Book 10: Endlessly Yours (Brooks & Rory)

The Falling for the Cassidy Brothers Series:
(Formerly the First Time Series)
Book 1: Good Time Boyfriend (Heath & Devney)
Book 2: Last Minute Fiancé (Luca & Addison)
Book 3: Second Chance Husband (August & Paisley)

Montgomery Ink Denver:
Book 0.5: Ink Inspired (Shep & Shea)
Book 0.6: Ink Reunited (Sassy, Rare, and Ian)
Book 1: Delicate Ink (Austin & Sierra)
Book 1.5: Forever Ink (Callie & Morgan)
Book 2: Tempting Boundaries (Decker and Miranda)
Book 3: Harder than Words (Meghan & Luc)

Book 3.5: Finally Found You (Mason & Presley)
Book 4: Written in Ink (Griffin & Autumn)
Book 4.5: Hidden Ink (Hailey & Sloane)
Book 5: Ink Enduring (Maya, Jake, and Border)
Book 6: Ink Exposed (Alex & Tabby)
Book 6.5: Adoring Ink (Holly & Brody)
Book 6.6: Love, Honor, & Ink (Arianna & Harper)
Book 7: Inked Expressions (Storm & Everly)
Book 7.3: Dropout (Grayson & Kate)
Book 7.5: Executive Ink (Jax & Ashlynn)
Book 8: Inked Memories (Wes & Jillian)
Book 8.5: Inked Nights (Derek & Olivia)
Book 8.7: Second Chance Ink (Brandon & Lauren)
Book 8.5: Montgomery Midnight Kisses (Alex & Tabby Bonus(
Bonus: Inked Kingdom (Stone & Sarina)

Montgomery Ink: Colorado Springs

Book 1: Fallen Ink (Adrienne & Mace)
Book 2: Restless Ink (Thea & Dimitri)
Book 2.5: Ashes to Ink (Abby & Ryan)
Book 3: Jagged Ink (Roxie & Carter)
Book 3.5: Ink by Numbers (Landon & Kaylee)

The Montgomery Ink: Boulder Series:

Book 1: Wrapped in Ink (Liam & Arden)

Book 2: Sated in Ink (Ethan, Lincoln, and Holland)
Book 3: Embraced in Ink (Bristol & Marcus)
Book 3: Moments in Ink (Zia & Meredith)
Book 4: Seduced in Ink (Aaron & Madison)
Book 4.5: Captured in Ink (Julia, Ronin, & Kincaid)
Book 4.7: Inked Fantasy (Secret ??)
Book 4.8: A Very Montgomery Christmas (The Entire Boulder Family)

The Montgomery Ink: Fort Collins Series:
Book 1: Inked Persuasion (Jacob & Annabelle)
Book 2: Inked Obsession (Beckett & Eliza)
Book 3: Inked Devotion (Benjamin & Brenna)
Book 3.5: Nothing But Ink (Clay & Riggs)
Book 4: Inked Craving (Lee & Paige)
Book 5: Inked Temptation (Archer & Killian)

The Promise Me Series:
Book 1: Forever Only Once (Cross & Hazel)
Book 2: From That Moment (Prior & Paris)
Book 3: Far From Destined (Macon & Dakota)
Book 4: From Our First (Nate & Myra)

The Whiskey and Lies Series:
Book 1: Whiskey Secrets (Dare & Kenzie)
Book 2: Whiskey Reveals (Fox & Melody)

ALSO FROM CARRIE ANN RYAN

Book 3: <u>Whiskey Undone</u> (Loch & Ainsley)

The Gallagher Brothers Series:
Book 1: <u>Love Restored</u> (Graham & Blake)
Book 2: <u>Passion Restored</u> (Owen & Liz)
Book 3: <u>Hope Restored</u> (Murphy & Tessa)

The Carr Family Series:
(Formerly the Less Than Series)
Book 1: Breathless With Her (Devin & Erin)
Book 2: Reckless With You (Tucker & Amelia)
Book 3: Shameless With Him (Caleb & Zoey)

The Fractured Connections Series:
Book 1: Breaking Without You (Cameron & Violet)
Book 2: Shouldn't Have You (Brendon & Harmony)
Book 3: Falling With You (Aiden & Sienna)
Book 4: Taken With You (Beckham & Meadow)

The Campus Roommates Series:
(Formerly the On My Own Series)
Book 0.5: My First Glance
Book 1: My One Night (Dillon & Elise)
Book 2: My Rebound (Pacey & Mackenzie)
Book 3: My Next Play (Miles & Nessa)
Book 4: My Bad Decisions (Tanner & Natalie)

ALSO FROM CARRIE ANN RYAN

The Ravenwood Coven Series:
Book 1: Dawn Unearthed
Book 2: Dusk Unveiled
Book 3: Evernight Unleashed

The Aspen Pack Series:
Book 1: Etched in Honor
Book 2: Hunted in Darkness
Book 3: Mated in Chaos
Book 4: Harbored in Silence
Book 5: Marked in Flames

The Talon Pack:
Book 1: Tattered Loyalties
Book 2: An Alpha's Choice
Book 3: Mated in Mist
Book 4: Wolf Betrayed
Book 5: Fractured Silence
Book 6: Destiny Disgraced
Book 7: Eternal Mourning
Book 8: Strength Enduring
Book 9: Forever Broken
Book 10: Mated in Darkness
Book 11: Fated in Winter

Redwood Pack Series:

ALSO FROM CARRIE ANN RYAN

Book 0.5: An Alpha's Path
Book 1: A Taste for a Mate
Book 2: Trinity Bound
Book 2.5: A Night Away
Book 3: Enforcer's Redemption
Book 3.5: Blurred Expectations
Book 3.7: Forgiveness
Book 4: Shattered Emotions
Book 5: Hidden Destiny
Book 5.5: A Beta's Haven
Book 6: Fighting Fate
Book 6.5: Loving the Omega
Book 6.7: The Hunted Heart
Book 7: Wicked Wolf

The Elements of Five Series:

Book 1: From Breath and Ruin
Book 2: From Flame and Ash
Book 3: From Spirit and Binding
Book 4: From Shadow and Silence

Dante's Circle Series:

Book 1: Dust of My Wings
Book 2: Her Warriors' Three Wishes
Book 3: An Unlucky Moon
Book 3.5: His Choice

Book 4: Tangled Innocence
Book 5: Fierce Enchantment
Book 6: An Immortal's Song
Book 7: Prowled Darkness
Book 8: Dante's Circle Reborn

Holiday, Montana Series:
Book 1: Charmed Spirits
Book 2: Santa's Executive
Book 3: Finding Abigail
Book 4: Her Lucky Love
Book 5: Dreams of Ivory

The Branded Pack Series:
(Written with Alexandra Ivy)
Book 1: Stolen and Forgiven
Book 2: Abandoned and Unseen
Book 3: Buried and Shadowed

ABOUT THE AUTHOR

Carrie Ann Ryan is the New York Times and USA Today bestselling author of contemporary, paranormal, and young adult romance. Her works include the Montgomery Ink, Redwood Pack, Fractured Connections, and Elements of Five series, which have sold over 3.0 million books worldwide. She started writing while in graduate school for her advanced degree in chemistry and hasn't stopped since. Carrie Ann has written over seventy-five novels and novellas with more in the works. When she's not losing herself in her emotional and action-packed worlds, she's reading as much as she can while wrangling her clowder of cats who have more followers than she does.

www.CarrieAnnRyan.com

EXTRAS

Want to go back and read the first generation and The Redwood Pack? You can begin the saga with A Taste for a Mate!

In the mood for a Romantasy that tugs at your heart and makes your heart pound? Try From Breath and Ruin!!

Love Fated Mates! Try the Dante's Circle series with Dust of My Wings that's full of mates, heat, and powerful enemies!

Fated Mate romances are the backbone of my reading and backlist and I'm so happy you're here!

If you'd like to read the next Generation with the Montgomery Ink Legacy Series: Bittersweet Promises

In the mood to read another family saga? Meet the Cage Family in The Forever Rule!

In the mood for more small town romance? Check out the Ashford Creek series with LEGACY. Or as I like to call it "The Small Town of Single Dads".

www.ingramcontent.com/pod-product-compliance
Lightning Source LLC
LaVergne TN
LVHW011758060526
838200LV00053B/3629